# A
# HUNTER'S
# MOON

This book is for Mrs Grace Caveney and
Mr Chris Wilson, with much love and all best wishes
for a long and happy marriage.

A Hunter's Moon is a uclanpublishing book

Text copyright © Danny Weston, 2021
Illustrations copyright © Shutterstock, 2021

978-1-912979-67-7

1 3 5 7 9 10 8 6 4 2

Set in 10/16pt Kingfisher by Amy Cooper.

A CIP catalogue record for this book is available from the British Library.

Printed and bound in Great Britain by Clays Ltd, Elcograf S.p.A.

Danny Weston

# A HUNTER'S MOON

uclanpublishing

Where there are sheep
the wolves are never far away
*Plautus*

# PROLOGUE

For perhaps the fourth time that night, Hamish Gilmour got up from the uncomfortable stool he'd been sitting on and walked over to the open door of the bothy. He gazed mournfully out across the deserted moorland. There had been bright moonlight earlier, and he'd easily been able to make out the splash of white that was the dead ram's fleece, lying on a ridge several hundred yards away to the east. But now thick clouds were moving in to obscure the moon, and he could scarcely make out any details.

The little shepherd's hut was bare and the stone chimney long since blocked up by a whole succession of birds' nests, so there was no hope of a fire tonight. Besides, the smell of woodsmoke might alert his quarry to his presence here. So he would just have to suffer the chill of the advancing darkness. He thought wistfully about his croft, less than a mile's walk from here and he pictured the big iron pan of broth, bubbling over a wood fire. He thought about his wife's delicious homemade bread and he pictured his two children, resisting their mother's call for them to go to bed and waiting hopefully for their father's return. But it could be a long time before he was able to head back. For a moment, his resolve weakened. He considered packing up his flintlock and trudging homewards before the rain began; because the smell of it was most definitely in the air, that strange, sulphurous tang that always preceded a storm. *Just my luck,* he thought. But he told himself, no, he'd lost two sheep in as many days and he could ill afford to lose any more to whatever it was that was preying on them.

He went reluctantly back to the stool and slumped down on it, running a hand through his thatch of dark hair and scratching at his ragged beard. His gangling frame made the rickety stool doubly uncomfortable; his long legs bent at an awkward angle. He thought again about finding the remains of the slaughtered ram this morning – a powerful adult – and how shocked he'd been at the state of it; how very mangled it was. It had resembled something he might expect to see on the counter of a butcher's shop, and he'd felt devastated by the loss. This had been a fine beast. It had required constant care and regular feeds and, what's more, he'd paid a pretty penny for it. His first thought was that it must have been killed by a wolf.

Oh, yes, he was well aware that everybody said that there were no wolves left in Scotland, that they were long gone even from the remotest areas of the Highlands, but what manner of dog – even a pack of them – could have done such damage to the poor creature? One thing was for certain, whatever had killed it had left enough meat to make it worth returning to and that was why Hamish had been waiting in the bothy for several hours now, passing the time in silence, waiting for the predator to return to the feast. Then all he needed was one clear shot.

As if in answer to the thought, a sound reached him: a prolonged howl. It started low and then rose in pitch and volume until it echoed eerily across the moor. It sounded uncomfortably close and despite himself, a chill ran through him. *Right*, he thought, *a wolf it most surely is*. People would hardly be able to argue its existence when he dragged its carcass into the market square tomorrow morning.

He took a deep breath and got up from the stool. Picking up the heavy flintlock rifle, he walked over to the doorway. As he stepped cautiously outside there was another sound, away to the east, a deep ominous rumble of thunder as the impending storm moved rapidly closer.

*Perfect*, he thought, but steeled his resolve. The beast seemed to be returning and he needed to be in position when it appeared. He must also act with caution, he reminded himself. There would probably only be time for one shot, but provided he managed to get it in before the rain fell and dampened his gunpowder, then he should be all right. He prided himself on being a decent marksman and there was no wolf that walked God's earth that could withstand a well-aimed lead ball. Hamish lifted the gun into a firing position and began to move slowly across the moor towards the ram's carcass, straining his eyes to get a visual fix on it.

Again, that eerie howl echoed in the night, sounding much closer now. Hamish looked all around him, but the visibility was bad and was getting worse by the moment. He tilted his head and gazed upwards, saw a broiling mass of cloud moving across the puny smear of light that was the moon. *Why now?* he wondered. It was as if something had it in for him.

Despite himself, Hamish's heart began to thud in his chest, the beat quickening as he got steadily closer to the carcass.

Once again, he considered turning back, but shook his head to dispel the thought. It had to end here and now. He would take no pleasure in ending the life of such a rare beast, but he simply could not afford to let his livelihood be taken away from him in this way. He kept putting one foot in front of the other and finally came to the low ridge, on top of which the ram had been lying. Only now, it didn't seem to be there. He frowned and toiled upwards. He crested the rise and stared down into the declivity beyond. Sure enough, there was a smudge of white down in the gully – the ram, lying on its side, but only half visible because a dark shape was crouched over it, as if inspecting it before it began to eat. It was the sheer size of the creature that caused Hamish to let out an involuntary gasp. Then, whatever it was raised its head to look up at him and Hamish's blood seemed to still momentarily in his veins.

In the darkness, he couldn't make out much detail but he heard the low, rumbling growl that issued from the creature, a sound that echoed the thunder he'd heard a moment earlier.

For an instant, he froze, staring down open-mouthed, teetering on the brink of panic. But then, the shocking realisation that the beast was already off the carcass and climbing the slope towards him, galvanised Hamish back into life. He snapped the rifle upwards, willing himself not to waste the shot. He needed to wait until the thing was so close, he couldn't miss. Now it was climbing towards him at a terrifying speed and his nerve broke. He lifted the rifle to his eye-line and aimed the sights between those two red orbs. He snatched in a breath and squeezed the trigger.

The weapon bucked in his hand, the stock punching against his shoulder and the smoke of the burning powder blew back into his eyes, temporarily blinding him. He blinked, coughed and shook his head, then stared apprehensively down into the gully. The ram still lay below him but of the creature that had been approaching, there was no sign. Hamish looked around in bewilderment. Where had it gone? At such close range, he surely couldn't have missed! Had the impact of the bullet flung it to one side?

He began to descend into the gully, looking cautiously to right and left and reaching instinctively for the powder horn that hung across his shoulder, meaning to reload the rifle, just in case he needed to put the beast out of its misery. But then something cold and wet splashed his face and he hesitated, realising that it was beginning to rain.

A heartbeat later, a giant hand plunged an invisible knife into the sky and ripped it wide open. The rain came down in icy rods, battering his head and shoulders and soaking through the thick fabric of his coat, chilling him to the bone. He stopped in his tracks, aware of his breath clouding in front of him and realising that it would be pointless now to try and reload the gun.

A deep rumble of thunder appeared to shake the very earth beneath his feet and he decided to head back to the meagre shelter of the bothy. As he turned, forked lightning split the sky and for a horrible instant, he saw that the creature was somehow perched on the top of the ridge that he had just descended and was gazing down at him, its eyes blazing like red hot coals, the rain bouncing up from its head and back to form a kind of iridescent halo. Hamish got a brief impression of its size, its open jaws, its long, shaggy, rain-slicked fur and he knew in that instant that it was no wolf. This was something beyond his ken.

Then darkness returned and he sensed, rather than saw, the beast hurtling down the slope towards him.

At the last moment, instinct made him turn the rifle around in his hands and hold it like a club, in a last desperate attempt to defend himself.

And then the thing was upon him. The last image he saw was of its hellish crimson eyes staring straight into his . . .

# CALLUM

The sound of metal-shod hooves clattering on cobbles awoke Callum suddenly from a disturbing dream. He'd been out alone on the moors at night, walking to an unknown destination. He'd crested a hill and gazed down into a valley where he saw the edge of a dense forest running from right to left across his field of vision, as far as the eye could see. There were lights shining in the midst of that forest; strange ethereal colours that blazed amidst the dense vegetation. As he stood there he'd felt the lights somehow pulling at him, exerting a powerful hold. And he knew in that moment that he wanted to go towards those lights – he wanted to walk in among the trees to discover the source of the colours . . .

He sat for a moment, befuddled, and then realised that he was sitting at the kitchen table. He must have drifted off in the middle of Old Mother McCloud's constant prattling, as she busied herself at the kitchen stove. He glanced guiltily up at her and saw that she was studying him, her wizened features arranged into a questioning look, her milky blue eyes staring accusingly at him. She must have just spoken to him, but he didn't have the first idea what she might have said.

'Er . . . I'm sorry,' he muttered. 'Did you . . .?'

'I said, you'd better shake yourself,' she snapped, in her croaky, dry-as-a-bone voice. 'You'll catch it if you keep him waiting any longer.'

Callum needed no second bidding. He had worked for Fraser McCloud for three months now and knew only too well the consequences of not following instructions the moment they were issued. Fraser had a harsh tongue and no qualms about using his fists whenever he felt his young assistant was being tardy.

At just fourteen years of age, this was Callum's first proper job, but he'd always imagined that when he did embark on such an enterprise, there'd be some kind of a wage to go along with it. All he got in return for his labours here were two of Mother McCloud's stodgy meals a day and a mangy, uncomfortable bed in the attic, where only total exhaustion compelled him to find any sleep. As to how long this wonderful job was going to last, that was anybody's guess.

He burst out of the kitchen door and into the yard, where he found Fraser sitting astride Mags, his chestnut mare, looking impatiently around. He was a tall, thin man, with straight black hair, which hung to his shoulders from beneath a wide brimmed hat. He wore a long, military style greatcoat and a pair of brown leather boots of which he was inordinately proud and which Callum was compelled to polish every evening. The cruel metal spurs that jutted from his heels were an indication of the kind of man he was. A former soldier – or so he claimed – he seemed to believe that everybody else in the world was somehow inferior to him and he had no problem announcing it to just about everyone he met. His young assistant was the lowest of the low, only here because his father was such a terrible card player and therefore worthy of no man's sympathy.

'What kept you?' snapped Fraser. He glared at Callum. 'You weren't sleeping, were you?'

'No, sir.' Callum stepped forward and caught Mags's bridle. He held her steady as Fraser swung himself down from the saddle and pulled the flintlock rifle from the leather holder at the back of it.

'Did you get that outhouse cleaned as I instructed?'

'Yes, sir.' This was true. Callum had scrubbed the filthy old place for hours, which probably accounted for the fact that he had fallen asleep at the table earlier.

'And do you have anything to report?'

Callum shook his head. 'All quiet,' he said. 'No visitors.' He knew that Fraser was hoping for offers of work, but in the time he'd been in the man's employ, he'd seen very little going on that might qualify for that description. Since being discharged from the army, Fraser seemed to be making his living by playing cards for money – something he was adept at – or taking a fee from various landowners in the area to help clear tenants out of properties they could no longer afford. He was, Callum supposed, a bully for hire, and he seemed to have few scruples about who he pushed around, provided somebody lined his pockets in return.

'I'm going inside,' he announced. He handed Mags's reins to Callum. 'Get her unsaddled and fed – and I want you to wipe her down from head to foot before putting the brush to her. I'll be back to check,' he added, managing to make it sound like a threat.

Callum nodded. He turned and led Mags dutifully over to the little stable. He unbolted the door and took her inside and into the stall next to Molly, an aging black mare that mostly served as Fraser's packhorse. Callum removed Mags's saddle and bridle and then scrubbed her down with handfuls of straw, before applying a course brush to her coat. As he worked, he talked to her and, as ever, she seemed to be listening to him.

'I keep telling myself,' he murmured, 'that one of these days, Mr McCloud will come and tell me that the debt has been paid. That I can go home again. But each day comes and goes, and he says nothing ...'

It galled him to think that his parents' croft was only a few miles away, and yet he hadn't been allowed to pay them a visit in all the time he'd been working here. He carried a vivid memory of the day he'd taken his leave of them. His mother's face, pale and red-eyed as she handed him a wrapped parcel of food for the journey – and his father, watching sullenly from a distance, too ashamed to even look his son in the eye after what had happened. Callum had no idea how much money had been lost in that fateful card game but he assumed it was a tidy sum, certainly more than his father could afford to lose.

It made Callum angry to think that his old man could have been so reckless, so stupid, when the family was already struggling to earn enough money to pay their monthly rent on the croft. But he also knew that his father hated to show the world how poor he was, and how he liked to play the big man whenever he was out with his drinking friends. Fraser would have seen that weakness and exploited it, coaxing Callum's father to raise the bet higher and higher until there was no backing down ...

Callum was surprised to discover that his shoulders were now moving rhythmically up and down ... and then there was the familiar feel of hot tears coursing down his cheeks. He pushed his face up against Mags's flank to muffle the sound of his sobs. She snorted and tossed her head, as if sympathising with his plight.

After a while, the tears subsided and he wiped his face on the sleeve of his jacket. Pointless to stand here feeling sorry for himself, he thought. He inspected Mags closely, terrified that he might have missed a bit of dried mud or a speck of gorse, but she looked perfect. He put out some feed for her and fetched a bucket of clean water from the pump in the yard, then closed the stable door and headed back to the house.

When he stepped into the kitchen he saw that Fraser was seated at the top end of the table wolfing down a large portion of meat stew, into which he was dipping a hunk of soda bread. Callum felt his stomach gurgle and he looked hopefully at Mother McCloud who was still stationed at the stove. She in turn glanced at her son.

'Am I to give the boy his ration?' she asked.

Fraser paused for a moment, as if considering the idea. He looked at Callum. 'You've given Mags a proper brush down?' he asked.

'Yes, sir.'

'I'll not find your work unsatisfactory?'

'No, sir, I don't believe so.'

'Go on then.' Fraser motioned to an empty seat at the far end of the table, then looked at his mother. 'Give him a decent portion,' he warned her. 'He'll need to keep his strength up.'

Callum almost winced at that. Who knew what arduous tasks Fraser had lined up for him? He seated himself and watched as

Mother McCloud heaped a ration of stew into a clay bowl and tore a chunk of bread from the new loaf. She brought it over, her ancient figure stooped and wasted, and set it down in front of him. 'There, now,' she said. 'Eat up.'

'Thank you kindly, Mother McCloud,' said Callum, knowing that if he didn't say something the meal would almost certainly be snatched away from him. He waited until she had returned to the stove before starting on the food, tearing wolfishly at the bowl's viscous contents.

'What's the great hurry?' snarled Fraser disapprovingly, and with an effort, Callum made himself slow down. He looked along the table at his employer, wondering if he dared ask the question he'd been wanting to ask for weeks. Fraser seemed to sense this and looked up from his own food. 'Well?' he enquired. 'Something on your mind?'

'Begging your pardon, sir, but I was just wondering . . .'

'Oh, you were, were you? That's an unfortunate habit of yours, boy. We've had words about that before, have we not?'

'Yes, sir, we have, but . . . if you please, I was wondering if you had any idea how much longer you might need to keep me here.'

Fraser smirked unpleasantly. '*Keep* you here?' He studied Callum for a moment in silence. 'Am I sensing some dissatisfaction? Are you not enjoying your time as my assistant?'

'Er . . . well, yes, of course, but . . .'

'Then there's no need for the question, is there?'

Callum looked at Fraser, dismayed, realising that he was already in danger of incurring the man's wrath. 'But . . . if you please, sir, I haven't seen my parents for a very long time.'

Fraser sniggered. 'In the case of your father, that should be considered a blessing,' he said. 'The man is an idiot who thinks he has an aptitude for cards but cannot keep a poker face to save his life. Your mother, on the other hand, I can see that might be something a person would miss. She is indeed fair to look upon, is she not?'

Callum didn't know what to say to that.

Fraser gave his bowl a last wipe with the remaining bread and pushed it into his mouth, then chewed noisily until it was gone. 'It's ridiculously simple, really,' he said at last. 'Allow me to explain. The day your father comes to me and pays me what he owes, that's when you shall be allowed to go home.'

Callum nodded. 'I understand that, sir. But . . . I have worked for three months, so . . . I suppose the sum owed must be less than it was before.'

Now Fraser threw back his head and laughed, before meeting Callum's gaze again. 'Forgive me,' he said. 'You are just a boy. You cannot be expected to know how these matters work. Perhaps you didn't appreciate that a debt incurs monthly interest.'

'Interest, sir?'

'Yes, interest. So, you see, your efforts here only serve to keep the debt at the same amount.'

'The . . . same amount?' Callum struggled to understand. 'You're saying . . .?'

'That the money owed is exactly the same as it was the day your father stumbled away from that card table. So unless his fortunes change dramatically, I'd say you're here for the long run.'

Callum stared at him, the food in his stomach suddenly turned to cold sludge. He was about to say something else, when the urgent sound of horses' hooves and the clatter of iron-bound wheels shattered the silence. They both turned to look out of the window. A fine black carriage was pulling into the courtyard pulled by a team of equally handsome grey horses.

'Hello, hello,' murmured Fraser. 'Who's this coming a-calling? Somebody with money, by the look of those wheels.' He turned back and glared at Callum, who was still sitting there open-mouthed in dismay. 'Well, what are you waiting for, lad?' he snapped.

Callum looked at him, still in shock. 'Sir?' he murmured.

'Go and see what they want!' snapped Fraser.

And Callum hurried to obey him.

# 2

# A VISITOR

When Callum stepped out into the yard, the carriage had already come to a halt. The driver had opened the door and was helping its single occupant down on to the cobbles. This was an elderly man, dressed in expensive-looking clothes – a brocaded coat with a matching waistcoat beneath, knee-length breeches and fancy leather shoes with silver buckles. He saw Callum standing there and smiled.

'Ah, hello,' he said.

'Good day to you, sir,' said Callum politely, bowing his head as Fraser had taught him. 'May I be of assistance?'

'You can start by telling me if I've come to the right place,' said the man. 'I'm seeking a Mr McCloud?'

'Oh, yes indeed, sir. He's inside. I'll take you to him directly.'

The man smiled. 'We've had quite a job locating this place,' he said, casting his gaze doubtfully over the modest farmhouse. 'I was expecting something . . . grander.' He turned back to look at his driver. 'Wait here for me, Michael,' he said. 'This shouldn't take long.'

'Very good, sir.' The tall, thin coachman bowed his head and then clambered back up on to his seat.

'May I enquire, what is your name?' asked Callum.

'I'm Colonel Chivers,' said the man. He looked puzzled. 'You are Mr McCloud's son?' he inquired.

'Oh, no, sir, his assistant. Please follow me.' Callum turned back, opened the door and led the old man inside, noting as he did so that the bowls and drinking vessels had been quickly cleared away from the table. Fraser was now sitting upright, his jacket neatly buttoned, doing his level best to look like a respectable fellow. Mother McCloud waited politely beside the stove.

'This is Colonel Chivers,' announced Callum.

Fraser indicated an empty seat next to him. 'Please, sir, make yourself comfortable,' he said.

'Thank you.' The colonel settled himself into the chair and looked quickly around the room, his face expressionless. Callum found himself thinking that the colonel was clearly used to more opulent surroundings.

Fraser motioned to Callum to take the seat at the far end of the table and he did as he was bid, noting with a twinge of disappointment that his unfinished bowl of stew was nowhere to be seen.

Fraser turned back to his visitor. 'May I offer you a dram of whisky, sir?'

'Oh, no need,' the colonel assured him. 'I'm not really a drinking man. Not these days, anyway.' He glanced across at Mother McCloud who was skulking in the background. 'Water will suffice,' he assured her, and she hurried off to fetch it. Callum settled himself in his chair and felt strangely as though he was looking at some kind of a play. Fraser was being quite unlike himself, attempting to give an impression of respectability – something that fit him awkwardly. He glanced towards the window. 'That's a fine-looking carriage,' he observed. 'Has it brought you far?'

'From Kinloch,' said the colonel. 'Near Loch Rannoch. A fair enough distance, I suppose.' He settled himself more comfortably in the chair and sighed. 'Travelling becomes more of a trial as you grow older,' he said. 'The bones ache more easily.'

Mother McCloud shambled back to the table with a mug of water and set it carefully down in front of the colonel. She bowed, then shuffled away again. 'Thank you, madam,' said the colonel. He lifted the mug and took a polite sip.

'So, I wonder what brings you all the way out here?' asked Fraser.

'I was looking for you, of course. You were recommended to me. Highly recommended, I might add.'

Fraser smiled thinly at this. 'I'm glad to hear of it,' he said. 'May I enquire who was singing my praises?'

The colonel waved a hand. 'I'm afraid I've quite forgotten,' he said. He gave a sly wink. 'Probably something to do with my advancing years.'

Again, Fraser gave that grudging smile, the closest he ever came to looking amused. 'And how may I be of assistance to you?'

'I have a proposition,' said Colonel Chivers. 'It's a matter that requires a man with certain skills. I was quite unable to find anybody suitable closer to home, so I ventured south. I'm told you have a strong nerve and considerable abilities with a rifle. You're a former military man, I understand.'

'That is correct.' Fraser nodded. 'We have that much in common, at least.' He frowned. 'If it's a matter of some tenants that you need evicting, I have plenty of experience in that regard.'

'Oh, no!' Colonel Chivers assured him. 'No, it's nothing like that. Actually, I am on very good terms with the tenants on my estate. My intention is to help them in a certain matter.' He set down his mug. 'I should explain. They are mostly sheep farmers, Mr McCloud. Hardworking, God-fearing, salt of the earth – I'm sure you know the sort. But, for the past couple of weeks, they have been tormented. You see, something has been preying on their livestock, some kind of ... wild animal.'

'I see.'

'It comes at night and . . . well, it makes quite a mess of whatever it goes after. There have been more than a dozen animals butchered so far. The tenants are much perturbed and demanding that I do something about the situation.' He shrugged his shoulders. 'But I'm afraid my soldiering days are long behind me. Since the death of my wife, some years ago, I prefer to spend my evenings with a good book in front of a roaring fire.'

'I understand,' said Fraser. 'You prefer to delegate such tasks. And I'm sorry for your loss.' He seemed to consider for a moment. 'So, it sounds as though you have a wolf problem. I'm sure that's something I can help with.'

'Hmm.' Colonel Chivers looked troubled. 'Except, of course, that everybody says there *are* no wolves left in the wild. It's a matter of public record that Sir Ewen Cameron shot the last Scottish wolf in Killiecrankie, very close to my estate, more than twenty years ago.'

Fraser looked unimpressed. 'It's easy to *say* that you've killed the last wolf, but a hard thing to prove. I've spoken to many people who claim to have heard them howling in the night. Why, only the other day, I ...'

'Whatever it is,' interrupted Colonel Chivers impatiently,

'I want it killed. As quickly as possible. I've wasted quite a bit of time trying to find somebody in my locality who can handle the situation.'

Fraser spread his hands in a dismissive gesture. 'Rest assured,' he said, 'provided we can come to an agreement on the price, I've no hesitation in putting myself forward for the task. I only—'

He broke off as Colonel Chivers reached into the inside pocket of his jacket and took out a piece of paper. He put it down on the tabletop and slid it across in front of Fraser. 'Those are my terms,' he said.

Fraser's eyebrows arched in surprise. He let out a low whistle. 'You really do want this done, don't you?' he said. He thought for a moment. 'You understand, it might take a wee while to track down the creature and kill it? I can't promise it shall be accomplished overnight.'

'All I ask is that you do it as quickly as you can,' said the colonel. He pointed at the paper. 'That sum is a daily rate. And as you can see, there'll be a bonus when the job is done. Accommodation will be provided at the local inn, for you and ...' He glanced down the table to Callum. '. . . for your assistant, if you need him to be there.'

Callum had been hoping that he might be excused this mission; it sounded dangerous. But Fraser glanced along the table at him and nodded.

'Oh yes, he will accompany me,' he said. 'I need somebody to handle the fetching and carrying.' Then his eyes narrowed suspiciously. 'Forgive me, Colonel, but I feel there's something you're not telling me. You say you couldn't find anyone to take on the task in your own neighbourhood? That strikes me as unusual.

Most places have a hunter living nearby, or another ex-military man . . . so why travel so far to engage my services?'

The colonel looked uncomfortable. 'I was unable to convince anybody in my locality to take on the task. May I be frank?'

'Of course.'

'They are a superstitious bunch. There have been suggestions that this beast might not be quite what it seems.'

There was a long silence. Then Fraser chuckled softly.

'Seriously?' he murmured. 'You mean . . .?'

'There have been whisperings and mutterings that whatever the creature is, it might be of supernatural origin. Nonsense, of course, but to those who follow such logic, well . . . the beast appears to venture out from the Forest of Tay and there are some in my locality who believe that place to be . . .' He struggled to find the right word. '. . . enchanted.'

The colonel's words made Callum remember the dream he'd had only a short while earlier. The image was so powerful it caused him to speak out without thinking.

'Are their lights in the forest?' he asked. 'At night.'

Both men turned to look at him. Fraser had a cold smirk on his face, but Colonel Chivers looked unsettled.

'I've heard people make such claims,' he admitted. 'Of course, I pay them no heed. I am a man of reason and logic. But . . . why do you ask?'

'Oh, I saw something myself . . . in a dream.'

'A dream?' Fraser looked outraged at the very idea. 'What piffle.'

Colonel Chivers smiled. 'Oh, I quite agree,' he said. 'If we believed the nonsense we saw in our slumbers, where would we be?'

Callum was about to speak again, but the cold gaze that Fraser directed at him dissuaded him from saying anything else on the subject.

Fraser studied the old man for a moment. 'To me, it sounds perfectly straightforward,' he said. 'A wolf exists in the forest and is coming out to dine on your tenants' sheep. Nothing mysterious there. We'll see how he enjoys a diet of lead shot.'

Colonel Chivers smiled and nodded. 'Good for you,' he said. 'There is, however, something else I should probably mention. One of the shepherds, a man called Hamish Gilmour, decided to go after the creature himself.'

'And?' said Fraser, puzzled.

'Well, the fact is, he's gone missing. He went out late one night to wait by the remains of a ram that had been killed. This was almost a week ago. By all accounts he was a formidable fellow and, everyone claims, a very good shot. But he failed to return home that night and after some time, his wife raised the alarm. Men were sent out to search for him, but of Mr Gilmour there has been no sign.'

'I see . . .'

'Oh, chances are he's simply taken the opportunity to go off somewhere for reasons best known to himself, but of course, his absence has fed into the theories of those crackpots who believe in the supernatural.' Colonel Chivers rolled his eyes. 'I've no doubt he'll turn up sooner or later, probably suffering from a hangover.' He chuckled, then spread his hands. 'So, that's the job, in a nutshell, Mr McCloud. Track the wolf and put a stop to the slaughter. That is, if you feel you're man enough for the task.'

Fraser looked thoughtful for a moment and Callum found

himself hoping that he would reject the idea, but, typically, a determined look came to his face.

'I'm confident I can do what you require,' he said. 'Let's make an agreement.' He held out his hand and after a moment's hesitation, the colonel took it and shook it firmly. Then the older man reached into another pocket and took out a heavy-looking leather purse.

'There's a down payment for you,' he said. 'It will cover your expenses and so forth. You'll have the rest on completion of the job.' From yet another pocket he produced some papers. 'I've taken the liberty of writing down directions to the inn where you'll be staying. On the way there, you might care to call at the Gilmour's croft and have a word with his wife, to see if she has any information as to her husband's whereabouts.' He tapped the paper. 'Their home is here, you see, just a couple of miles from the inn.'

Fraser nodded. He took the purse and felt the weight of it, then smiled. 'The job's as good as done,' he said. 'We'll prepare our equipment tonight and set off first thing tomorrow morning.'

'Excellent.' Without further ado, Colonel Chivers stood up from the table. 'And now, if you'll forgive me, I'm afraid I must take my leave of you. There's a good distance to travel and I'd like to be home before nightfall.'

\*\*\*

Callum watched as the coach clattered noisily out of the courtyard. Colonel Chivers leant briefly out of the open window and gave him a regal wave. Callum frowned. Perhaps it was something to do with the dream he'd had, but he felt uneasy about this. Getting away from here ought to have been a blessing and yet, he couldn't rid himself of the conviction that he and Fraser would be going into danger.

When he stepped back into the kitchen, he saw that Mother McCloud had emerged from her usual kitchen lair and was standing beside Fraser, her hands on her hips.

'All I'm saying is, I don't like it,' Callum heard her say.

'You're being ridiculous,' Fraser told her. 'We'll be gone a few days, a week at the most. You'll be perfectly fine.' He patted the coin-stuffed purse on the tabletop. 'The good colonel is paying handsomely for my services. This is the best break I've had in ages, and I shan't let you spoil it. Don't worry,' he added. 'I'll leave you plenty of housekeeping. You won't go short.'

'I don't care about the money,' croaked Mother McCloud. 'You heard what he said. Supernatural! That's the very word he used.'

'Pah!' Fraser sneered at her. 'He told us that was what some simpletons in his neighbourhood are saying. You forget, Mother, times have moved on since your childhood days. Few people still put their belief in ghosts and hobgoblins.'

'Then you tell me why a man as wealthy as that one would be prepared to travel such a distance to engage the services of someone like *you*.'

Fraser considered her words. 'You heard what he said. I came highly recommended. He sought me out.'

Now it was her turn to laugh. 'You fool. I always said your vanity would be the destruction of you one day. Recommended by who? You think your reputation is that high?' She shook her head. 'Couldn't you see what I could?'

Fraser gazed up at her, puzzled. 'See what?' he murmured.

'That man was scared,' said Mother McCloud. 'He was scared out of his wits. But he put on an act and buttered you up and got you to shake him by the hand.' She turned away with a grunt of disgust. 'Which, in my book, makes you the biggest fool in the country.'

Fraser gazed after her a moment, a perturbed look on his face. Then he noticed Callum standing there, watching.

'What are you gawking at?' he snapped. 'Don't stand there catching flies. Go and pack your things. We leave at first light.'

# 3

# THE WASHER AT THE FORD

They rode away at dawn, the sky a sullen grey wash, the air full of fine drizzle. Fraser led the way on Mags and Callum did his level best to impersonate a horseman, hunched awkwardly on to Molly's ancient saddle, bags of equipment piled haphazardly around him.

After silently dispensing a breakfast of lumpen porridge, Mother McCloud stood in the doorway watching them leave – her arms crossed, her face a picture of resentment. As far as Callum was aware she and Fraser had passed no further conversation about the trip, but she didn't need to say anything. Disapproval seemed to spill from her every pore.

They rode through the nearest village and then headed out on to the narrow track that headed north towards Pitlochry. They travelled for hours in silence and as they went along, the weather gradually improved until by midday some weak sunlight was beginning to break through the clouds. The land inclined steadily upwards, becoming wilder and more forested with each mile they covered. Every so often, Fraser stopped to peruse the written instructions he'd been given, but he hardly spoke a word to Callum and the boy could tell that his employer was ill at ease.

Perhaps after his mother's words, he'd had time to reconsider Colonel Chivers's brisk and hurried manner when he'd visited – how intent he'd been on getting an agreement, how quickly he'd agreed to pay out even if it took a while to locate and kill the mysterious beast. The man was evidently wealthy but, in Callum's scant experience, wealthy people were the ones who watched their expenses most carefully. It was how they had got to be rich in the first place.

In the late afternoon, Fraser and Callum crested a ridge and found themselves looking down at a winding, fast-flowing stream that cut like a serpent through the green landscape below them. On a shingle bank, beside a shallow crossing place, a woman was kneeling, washing clothes, her head covered and her back turned to them. Fraser studied his written instructions for a moment, then shook his head.

'By my reckoning, we should be drawing close to the shepherd's croft, but I'm confused. It says nothing about crossing water.' He pointed down to the stream. 'Go and ask that woman if she can offer us some directions.'

Callum felt some reluctance to do this. He wasn't good with strangers, he always felt awkward when speaking to them. At the same time, he had worked for Fraser long enough to know that he never backed down over anything – so he tapped his heels into Molly's flanks and urged her down the slope to the river. When he got to the water's edge, he swung himself clumsily down from the saddle, not wanting to risk his mount's hooves on the slippery shingle. He let out a quiet groan as he felt the cramps in his legs and buttocks send shocks of pain through him, making him feel like an old timer, but he stretched himself and put one foot in front of the other, his boots crunching on the loose stones.

The woman continued with her work as he approached, her hands swirling something in what must have been icy cold water.

'Good day to you, missus,' he said, expecting her to pause and look back at him – but she ignored his greeting. Perhaps she was deaf, he thought, or simply lost in her own thoughts. As he got closer, he realised that she was humming a tune under her breath, a strangely familiar melody that he couldn't quite place. He continued to move closer and when he was just a few steps away from her, he tried again. 'Madam?' he ventured. 'I wonder if you could direct me to the croft of a man called Hamish Gilmour?'

Finally, she became aware of his presence. She stopped humming and half-turned to look at him. He saw that she had a scarf wrapped across the lower part of her face. The eyes that regarded him were a strange, golden-brown in colour, staring with an intensity that made him feel uncomfortable. She stopped swirling the clothing and lifted up a dripping hand to point across the ridge where Fraser was waiting.

'It's only a wee distance in that direction,' she hissed. Her voice was muffled by the scarf, but had a strange, course quality to it that sounded unnaturally loud to Callum's ears; her words almost seemed to echo over the sound of rushing water. But his attention had been drawn to her hand, which looked decidedly strange to him. In the brief moment that it was in sight, before it was plunged back under the surface of the water, he'd registered that the fingers of that hand were webbed, translucent flaps of blue skin stretched between each of them.

Then the woman spoke again. 'Ride for a half mile and you'll see a narrow track leading away to your left. Follow it and you'll soon come to the croft. Such a tragedy there. Such sorrow. Poor Hamish. We all weep for him.'

Callum swallowed. 'He's . . . missing,' he said. 'We've come to look for him.'

'Aye. Missing. And you've had such a long journey to get here.' Her hands swirled a garment in the rushing water. 'Mind you, the weather's a lot better now than when you set off. And the old woman's porridge will have sustained you.'

Callum stared down at her in amazement, wondering how she could possibly know so much.

'Do you . . .?' He hesitated to ask her another question, but felt he needed to. 'Do you have any idea what happened to Mr Gilmour?' he ventured.

A long sigh from the woman. 'Ah, he is with them now,' she murmured.

'Them?'

The hooded head nodded. 'The walkers in the woods. The hiders in the trees. They have prepared a bed for him in the forest.'

Callum didn't have the first idea what she was talking about, but he knew that he really didn't want to tarry here any longer. 'Well, er . . . thank you,' he said. 'We'll be on our . . .'

He stopped talking. His gaze had moved down to the surface of the clear water and he could see the garment she was holding. It was swirling about in the current; a plain white shirt, its sleeves twisting and turning. He could also see the crimson tendrils that were spilling out from it and flowing downstream in thick clouds.

He stared at them, wide-eyed, thinking that they must surely stop in a moment, but there seemed to be no end to them. He looked downstream and saw that the whole river was stained red.

And then the woman started singing, crooning in a low voice.

*'Poor Johnny he's a-sleepin'*
*The moonlight comes a-creepin'*
*And all his children gather now*
*To sing their last goodbyes.*

*And in the glen the weepin'*
*Their promise they are keepin'*
*To bid poor Johnny fare thee well*
*As tears spill from their eyes.'*

Callum felt something jolt through him, a cold, juddering sliver of pure terror that made his breath catch in his throat. He didn't say anything else, just turned and hurried back across the shingle to Molly, who he could see looked skittish, as though she could smell the fear coming off him.

He grabbed the pommel of the saddle and scrambled up into it, nearly kicking off half the baggage in his haste. He got Molly turned around and rode back up the slope at speed. He glanced back just once to see that the woman was now lifting the garment up from the water as if to inspect it. Even at this distance, he could see how stained with red the white fabric was.

He turned back and urged Molly onwards. He came up level with Fraser and didn't slow down.

'Well?' Fraser shouted after him.

'This way!' shouted Callum, and led Fraser in the direction the woman had indicated.

'What's the damned hurry?' asked Fraser. 'Did the woman say something to you?'

'She gave me directions.' That was all Callum said, and he didn't speak again until they'd turned on to the track she'd mentioned and the outline of the croft had come into view.

Finally, Callum pulled Molly to a halt. Fraser came alongside him and gave him a querulous look.

'What's gotten into you, boy?' he snapped. 'You took off like the very devil was snapping at your heels.'

Callum stared into the distance, still seeing the woman's weirdly coloured eyes gazing into his. 'It's just that the old woman scared me,' he murmured.

'Her?' Fraser looked baffled. 'She looked like some old fishwife. What did she say to you that was so unsettling?'

'She . . . sang a song to me.'

Fraser gave him an odd look. 'That doesn't sound particularly menacing,' he said.

'You needed to be there,' whispered Callum.

'Whisht.' Fraser shook his head and clambered down from Mags. He handed his reins to Callum and walked briskly towards the door of the croft, a low, white-painted building with a thatched roof. A few sorry-looking chickens pecked at scraps of corn in the cobbled yard and he swung a boot at one that was in his way.

'Let's see if we can get some answers here,' he said.

And he lifted a hand to knock.

# 4
# THE CROFT

The woman who came to the door looked exhausted, Callum thought. She was pale and thin, and her blonde hair hung in forlorn straggles on either side of her face. Her blue eyes were ringed with red as though she had shed considerable amounts of tears recently or had not slept, most likely a combination of the two. She looked at Fraser with disappointment and it was clear she'd been expecting – or at least, hoping – to see somebody else. But she remembered her manners and bowed her head politely.

'Good day to you, sir,' she said.

'Mrs Gilmour?' ventured Fraser.

She nodded.

'I am Fraser McCloud. I have been enlisted by Colonel Chivers to take care of your wee problem.'

'My . . . problem?' she echoed.

'I refer of course to the beast that's been preying on your livestock. I'm sure you'll be relieved to hear that I have been sent here to kill it.'

She gazed at him blankly and he continued.

'Rest assured, I shall give the matter my swift attention. But the colonel thought it might be an idea if we called by and asked you a few questions about your husband. May we come in?'

'Yes, of course.' The woman stepped obediently back from the door and Fraser gestured to Callum to dismount. He climbed gratefully down from the saddle and tethered both horses to a stout wooden rail that stretched along the front of the croft. Then he followed Fraser into the building.

It was a humble-looking place – small, and lit only by the light from a single window. There was a hard earth floor and a quartet of spindly chairs. At a battered pine table, two young children sat side-by-side. There was a little girl, blonde like her mother, who might have been five or six years old. She was playing with a doll, a soft homemade poppet with an expressionless face and gangling pink limbs. The girl's companion looked to be a couple of years older; dark-haired and stocky, but his features were close enough to hers to announce that he was her older brother. He was gazing blankly ahead, staring at a wall and taking no notice of the visitors.

'You must forgive my son,' said the woman. 'He is consumed with worry for his father.' She went to the table and stooped so her head was level with those of her children. 'Moira, Angus . . . why don't you go outside, the pair of you, and play in the yard?' They got up from their chairs without a word and went to the door. As they walked past Callum, the boy glanced briefly up at him and he saw the worry in the lad's brown eyes. Callum gave him what he hoped was an encouraging smile, but Angus seemed to look right through him.

'Mind now, don't go far from the house,' the children's mother warned them. 'Stay close.' Then they were stepping outside, closing the door behind them. The woman gave Fraser an apologetic look.

'I'm sorry, sir, I have no refreshment to offer you other than a mug of water, if you would like it.'

Fraser made a dismissive gesture with one hand. 'It's of no consequence,' he said gruffly. 'What do people call you?'

'Shona, sir. Please, won't you sit down?' She indicated the chairs that her children had just vacated and Fraser and Callum did as she suggested, Callum trying not to wince as he lowered his saddle-sore backside on to the wood. Shona pulled over another chair and settled herself on the far side of the table, facing her visitors.

'So,' said Fraser. 'Colonel Chivers tells me that your husband went out a week ago . . .'

'Six days,' she corrected him. 'In the evening. I didn't want him to go. I pleaded with him. After what people had been saying, it seemed reckless to go out at night, alone, but that's Hamish for you.' Despite her worry, the ghost of a smile flickered across her face. She was evidently proud of her husband's stubbornness.

'And what exactly *have* people been saying?' Fraser asked her.

'That this creature that has been preying upon our sheep is not a wolf but a *Cù Sìth*.'

'A . . . *coo shee*?' Fraser stared at her, uncomprehending. 'What is that when it's at home?'

'The hound of the trows.'

Fraser glared at her.

'The trows?' he echoed. 'I don't . . .'

'The people of the woods,' she elaborated, saying it quietly as though afraid of being overheard.

Her words reminded Callum of something the woman at the ford had said. 'Do you mean, the . . . *walkers* in the woods?' he murmured.

'Aye, some call them that! Of course, Hamish said that was nonsense. "Show me the creature that can stand up to the Thunderer," he said. That was what he called his gun.' She shook her head. 'I said to him, "Hamish, at least round up some of the other crofters and take them along with you. There are plenty hereabouts who would stand beside you if you only said the word and many you have helped out in tricky situations before." But no, off he went into the night, promising he'd be back by morning. Only he never returned.'

Fraser frowned. 'The colonel said he might have gone off drinking with friends ... that he'd probably show up sooner or later.'

Shona looked offended at the very idea. 'Hamish is no drinking man,' she retorted. 'Oh, perhaps a mug of ale on special days, but no more than that. He cannot afford it, for one thing.'

Callum found himself thinking of his father, who clearly had never learnt to follow such simple logic.

'I cannot imagine why the colonel should make such an accusation if he didn't believe it to be a possibility,' said Fraser.

'And I'm telling you, sir, that is not my husband's way.'

Fraser frowned. 'If you say so. I'm told that there was a search for him.'

'Aye, sir. I went out first and then others came out to look. In the end, half of the community came to help.'

'And yet the colonel said no trace of him was found.'

Now Shona looked angry. 'I'm aware that's what he's been telling people,' she snapped. 'But it's no' the truth.' She glanced guiltily towards the door of the house as if to ascertain that her children weren't about to come back in, then got up from her seat. 'One moment, please,' she said. She went to a cupboard set into one wall of the house and, pulling it open, she drew out a long object wrapped in canvas. She carried it back to the table and laid it down in front of Fraser. 'I found this,' she said. 'Near to what was left of Hamish's dead ram.'

Fraser reached out his hands and started to undo the ties that held the parcel closed.

'My children haven't seen it,' Shona warned him. 'I couldn't bear to show it to them. I'd rather you didn't mention it in front of them.'

Fraser paused to look at her for a moment and then pulled back the fabric to reveal a flintlock rifle – or, at least, the remains of one. The wooden stock had been completely shattered, as though struck by prodigious force. What's more, the stout iron barrel was bent completely out of shape. Callum couldn't help but notice that the entire length of the weapon was spattered with drops of dried blood. Fraser let out a long, slow breath and Callum glanced up at him to see a look of realisation on his sallow face. It had clearly just dawned on him why the colonel had been prepared to travel such a distance to find somebody to take care of his little 'wolf' problem.

'Colonel Chivers surely couldn't have known of this,' murmured Fraser.

'Oh, but he did,' Shona corrected him. 'I took the gun straight over to him myself. I rode up to that fancy house of his on the moors and showed it to him, just as I'm showing it to you. This is The Thunderer, given to Hamish by his father. It's one of his most treasured possessions. That gun has survived several battles. Now look at it.'

'What did the colonel say?' asked Callum. 'When you showed him this?'

'He asked who else knew of it. I said I was alone when I found it and that I hadn't shown it to the other crofters yet. He told me not to. He said that if I did it would only cause more mutterings, more panic.' She looked shamefaced now. 'He even . . .' She looked down at the shattered gun, her face reddening. 'He even offered me money to keep its existence to myself.' She shook her head. 'I wanted to tell him no, that I would never do that, but, God forgive me, I took the money. I was desperate, sir. The weans have to eat and there's no money coming into this house. What else was I to do? But . . . you are not crofters, so . . . I am showing you this in the hope you'll be able to do something about it.' She reached out and carefully re-tied the wraps around the flintlock, clearly worried that her children might come back in and catch sight of it.

Fraser leant back in his chair. 'I should have been made aware of this,' he muttered. 'From the very start. I should have been given the full story.' He stared at the covered rifle for a few moments. 'But this only proves that a powerful beast attacked your husband. A wolf. Not a . . . what did you call it? A coo . . .?'

'A *Cù Sìth*, sir. That's what some of the older crofters are calling it anyway. They say it is the beast that the people of the woods summon to avenge them.'

'Avenge them? For what?' sneered Fraser. 'For stepping on the grass?'

'No, sir. Much more than that. For cutting down the trees around their sacred home. That was Colonel Chivers's doing. He wants to build on the land, so he paid some foresters to go into the woods and—'

Fraser stood up from the table, his expression hostile. 'I'm not listening to any more of this nonsense,' he protested.

'It's heathen talk! You and the others would do better to spend your time reading the Holy Bible.' He gestured to Callum to get to his feet. 'Come on,' he said. 'Let's ride on to the inn and see if we can get more sense out of the people there.'

Shona looked wounded. 'I only tell you what others have told me,' she said. 'All I know is, my husband was taken from me and Colonel Chivers does not want the story to get out. What does that say to you, sir?'

'It says nothing,' insisted Fraser. 'Only that some people have let their imaginations run away with them. Good day to you, Madam. Rest assured, I shall find the beast that attacked your husband and I shall kill it. Then we'll see what your superstitious friends have to say about that.'

He walked to the door, opened it and stepped outside. Callum lingered a moment, gazing apologetically at the woman. 'You'll have to forgive him,' he said quietly. 'He's . . .'

'. . . afraid,' finished Shona. 'Aye. Just like all the others.'

Callum shrugged and went outside. He found Fraser standing with his back to the door, his hands on his hips, gazing out across the moorland to a distant range of pale blue mountains. The two children were kneeling on the ground nearby. The girl was talking in a low voice to her doll, but her brother was also staring into the distance, as though hopeful he'd spot a familiar figure approaching.

Callum unhitched the horses and handed Mags's reins to Fraser. 'You know,' he said quietly. 'You could always return the money to Colonel Chivers and tell him you don't want the job.'

Fraser gave him a blistering look. 'Are you mad?' he snapped. 'Why would I do a thing like that?'

He clambered up into his saddle. Wearily, Callum followed his example. As they rode away, he was aware of Shona's gaze. She was watching them bleakly from the doorway of the croft. Callum rode on for some distance and when he finally glanced back, she and her children had gone back inside and the door was tight shut against the outside world.

# 5

# THE LANDLORDS'S PALE-EYED DAUGHTER

The sun was setting, suffusing the western horizon with a blood-red glow, by the time they reached the Shepherd's Crook.

It was a big, rambling inn on the outskirts of the village, the rough plastered walls painted white. There was a stable beside the main building so Fraser and Callum dismounted there and handed their horses over to the care of the ostler, a skinny old man who barely spoke a word to them.

'We're expected,' said Fraser. 'The landlord?'

The old man pointed out through the open doors and turned to lead the horses into some vacant stalls, so Fraser and Callum gathered up their bags and walked across the cobbled courtyard to the inn's main entrance. They climbed a low flight of stone steps, went in through the open oak doors and found themselves in a large, low-ceilinged room where a log fire was already blazing in a massive hearth. Behind a counter, a short, heavyset man with a ruddy face and a neat brown wig, offered them a welcoming smile. He wore an apron that had once been white but was now smeared with a whole series of different coloured stains, from bright yellow to dark red.

'You must be Mr McCloud,' he said, in a deep, booming voice.

'That's me, sure enough,' agreed Fraser.

'The colonel told me you'd be dropping by this evening.' The man studied Callum for a moment. 'And this would be your assistant?'

'That's correct,' said Fraser.

'A warm welcome to ye both. I'm Andrew Sessions, the landlord of the Shepherd's Crook. Let me get you some mugs of ale, I'm sure you must have worked up a fierce thirst on such a long ride.'

'Sounds good,' said Fraser.

'I'm afraid the mutton pie isn't quite ready yet, but I dare say you'll both appreciate a helping of that once it's done.'

'We won't say no,' said Callum eagerly. He was very hungry after the long trip and wanted to be sure he wasn't left out.

Fraser shot him a critical look. 'Watch your manners,' he said.

'Oh, no, that's fine, we don't stand on ceremony here,' insisted Andrew. 'Put those heavy bags down and make yourselves comfortable.'

The two visitors were happy to comply with the request. They moved over to a table and settled themselves into chairs. Fraser glanced quickly around the deserted room. 'Where is everybody?' he asked.

"Oh, it's early yet. I expect we'll have a few of my regulars along in due course.' Andrew lowered his voice, as if confiding a secret. 'I have to admit, our recent troubles have not been exactly good for business. Hopefully that's something you'll be able to remedy.' He dipped a metal jug into an open barrel and dispensed ale into two large tankards. He stepped out from behind the counter and brought the drinks over to the table. 'Now, drink hearty good sirs and let me know what you think of our local brew. It's my own recipe.'

Callum took an eager gulp of the ale, which was bitter and malty with a considerable kick. He felt very grown up being encouraged to drink ale in such a reckless fashion. Fraser lowered his own tankard, a line of white foam across his top lip. 'It's good,' he said. 'Just what was needed.'

'There's plenty more where that came from,' Andrew assured him. 'You just let me know when you want a refill. I promised the colonel I'd take very good care of you both.' He smiled. 'I trust you had an uneventful journey.'

'A steady ride,' said Fraser. 'I'd say we're both a little saddle sore.' He studied the landlord over the rim of his tankard for a moment and Callum was aware of him getting the measure of the man. 'We stopped at the Gilmour croft on the way here,' he continued 'I wanted to speak to the missing man's wife.'

'Ah . . .' Andrew nodded. He looked uncomfortable at this news. 'Poor woman,' he said. 'She must be beside herself with worry.'

Fraser nodded. 'I'd say she is. I'd also say the event has unhinged her. She has some fanciful notions.'

'Does she indeed?'

'Aye.' Fraser took another gulp of his ale. 'She told me that there are many people around these parts who believe the beast, whatever it turns out to be, isn't as straightforward as might be supposed.'

Andrew sighed and shook his head. 'I know it, sir. I've heard many customers, drinking of an evening, who share that same view.' He rolled his eyes. 'It's not something I subscribe to, if that's what you're asking.'

Fraser looked relieved. 'I'm glad to hear it, Mr Sessions. From what Mrs Gilmour said, I was beginning to think that everybody in these parts had the same belief. The woman spun me a yarn about the woods being enchanted . . .'

Andrew chuckled. 'Aye, well, I won't pretend I'm surprised. You must understand, Mr McCloud, that most people here grew up hearing such stories from their grandparents and took them as gospel. I'm from round these parts myself but, unlike many, I've travelled. I regularly visit Edinburgh, where such fanciful notions are treated with the contempt they deserve. But you see, Mr McCloud, to some people, such stories are as real as . . . this table.' He reached out a pudgy hand and patted its scratched surface.

'Mrs Gilmour said something about trees being chopped down,' said Callum, ignoring the sharp look that Fraser gave him. 'She said it was to blame for what's happened here.'

'Aye. Well, there has been some of that going on, for sure. The colonel wanted to clear a bit of his land for building purposes. He desires a hunting lodge in which to entertain guests. But he's surely entitled to do that, isn't he? After all, that's just progress.' He paused as though expecting a reply, but when he didn't get one, he continued hurriedly. 'Now, Mr McCloud, I've put you in one of the guest rooms on the first floor, at the front of the building. I'm sure you'll be more than comfortable there.' He glanced warily at Callum. 'And as the other rooms are spoken for, I hope your assistant won't mind if I put him in the hayloft, above the stable.

It's warm enough up there and the straw makes the finest bed a young man could ask for.'

Callum opened his mouth to reply, but Fraser answered for him. 'That will be perfectly suitable for him, Mr Sessions.'

'Excellent. Well, why don't I get you installed in the guest room, Mr McCloud, so you can have a wee rest before supper? And my daughter can show, er . . .' He looked puzzled. 'I didn't catch your name,' he said.

'It's Callum.'

'Very good.' Andrew turned and walked to an open doorway that led on to a hallway. 'Mhairi!' he called. 'Will you come here, please?'

After a short wait, a girl around Callum's age appeared in the doorway. She too was wearing a white apron, but hers was much cleaner than her father's. Callum tried not to stare at her. Mhairi had long, straight hair that hung past her shoulders, almost to her waist. The hair was as black as a raven's wing and her skin the colour of milk. But it was her eyes that drew his attention. They were pale red in colour and seemed to stare at Callum with a fierce intensity that unsettled him. She soon became aware of his discomfort and bobbed a quick curtsy.

'Good evening, sirs,' she said. 'Welcome to the Shepherd's Crook.'

'Mhairi, would you take young Callum here and show him the way up into the hayloft?' He pointed to the bags stacked in a corner. 'And give him a hand with his baggage.'

'I only have the one,' Callum told her, pointing to it. He swallowed down the rest of his ale and jumped to his feet, but Mhairi got to the bag before him and swung it easily on to her shoulder.

'Follow me,' she said, and led the way back to the entrance doors.

'Dinner will be in around an hour,' Andrew shouted after him. 'I'll give you a shout when it's ready. You can eat in here.'

'Thank you, sir!' Callum shouted back. He was already looking forward to tasting something that hadn't been prepared by Mother McCloud. The old woman had a tendency to overcook her meals until they had boiled down to a tasteless sludge. He followed Mhairi outside, down the steps and across the cobbled courtyard.

'So, you two are quite the celebrities,' said Mhairi, giving him a sly look over her shoulder.

'Are we?' Callum was puzzled.

'Of course. Everyone is talking about you and your father.'

Callum scowled. Why were so many people making that assumption? 'He's not my father, just my employer.'

'Oh, is that so?' she said. 'You look alike.'

'No,' said Callum, 'we do not.'

She chuckled. 'Touched on a nerve, have I? Seems we two have something in common, though. Andrew Sessions isn't my father, either.'

Callum was puzzled. 'He's not? But he calls you daughter.'

'Aye. That's his choice.' She waved a hand as if to dismiss the subject. 'Anyway, as I was saying, everyone hereabouts knows that you two have come here to save us from the *Cù Sìth*.'

'You mean the wolf,' Callum insisted.

'Do I?' Another shrug. 'If you say so.'

They went in through the open doors of the stable. The old ostler had just lit a lantern and was placing it on top of an old barrel, suffusing the place with a warm, welcoming wash of light. But as he turned to look at Mhairi, his expression was anything but welcoming. His wizened features arranged themselves into a furious scowl and he uttered three words at her.

'Here's the shargie!' he snarled. He waited a moment, presumably to see if there was any reaction from her but when he didn't get one, he stalked past her and Callum, out into the gathering darkness.

Callum gazed after him, puzzled.

'What was that about?' he asked.

Mhairi seemed unconcerned. 'Oh, ignore him. I do. Tam doesn't say much,' she said. 'And what he does say isn't usually very friendly.'

Callum looked at her. 'But what does it mean?' he asked. 'What he called you? "Shargie"?'

'Oh, that's just an old word for a foundling.' She noticed Callum's furrowed brow and explained. 'Like I said, Andrew isn't my father. Him and his wife found me when I was a bairn.'

'They *found* you?' Callum stared at her. 'Where?'

She studied him for a moment. In the glow of the lantern, those uncanny eyes looked even bigger than before.

'In the Forest of Tay,' she said. She indicated a wooden stepladder leading up through an open hatch. 'This way,' she told him and scrambled easily upwards.

But Callum stood for a moment, gazing up into the dark opening above him, wondering why his nerves were suddenly jittering and rattling like alarm bells in his head. A moment passed and then Mhairi's pale face loomed out of the shadow above, her expression mocking him. 'Well,' she murmured. 'What's keeping you? You're not afraid of the dark, are you?'

# 6

# DARK

Callum gathered his nerve and, placing a foot on the first rung of the ladder, he started to climb. It was only a few steps upwards before his head and shoulders plunged into the darkness of the loft. He hesitated a moment, unsure of what to do next. He couldn't see a thing. Then a cold hand closed tightly around his, pulling him forward.

'This way,' murmured Mhairi's voice. 'Don't worry, I've got you.'

'I-I can't see,' gasped Callum.

'No. It's no matter, your eyes will soon grow accustomed to it.'

She was right. Eventually, the glow from the lantern, spilling in through the open hatch, dimly illuminated the interior of the hayloft. He could just discern a thick carpet of straw stretching in front of him and there, crouched on her hands and knees, was Mhairi. She seemed to be enjoying his uncertainty.

'I love it up here,' she said. 'I used to play in the loft all the time when I was a bairn. I had a whole army of wee dolls and I used to create adventures for them.' A pause, then. 'How do you come to work for him?'

'*Him*?' Callum managed to get himself seated on a deep pile of straw.

'Mr McCloud, I mean. Are you an orphan too?'

'Oh, no, I have parents. But I live in Fraser's house.'

'Why's that? Did your parents get tired of you?'

'No, of course not. No, they . . .' Callum was reluctant to tell her the full story, so he simply said, 'They needed extra money, so I took a job.'

Mhairi seemed to consider this. 'So, you get paid for your work then? I mean, I work at the inn, but Andrew doesn't give me a wage.'

Again, Callum didn't feel inclined to offer her the whole truth. 'I just . . . work for Fraser McCloud. And it's not for ever. One day I'll go home to my parents.'

'You don't like him.' It wasn't a question, so much as a statement.

'What makes you say that?'

'I can tell these things. It's a gift I have. You don't like him because of . . . some kind of game.' She turned her head aside for a moment, then looked back at him. 'Cards,' she said. 'It's something to do with cards.'

He felt uncomfortable at her ability to read him so easily and made an attempt to change the subject. 'You said something about Mr Sessions and his wife . . . finding you?'

'That's right. Her name was Isla, but she died when I was wee. I don't really remember her.'

'May I ask what happened?' asked Callum awkwardly.

'She had a fever and, like fevers often do, it took her. Andrew doesn't talk about Isla much, but he always says she was bonnie. He did give me a wee keepsake with a portrait of her in. I have it in a safe place. I'll show you some time if you like.'

There was silence for a moment and he strained to get a better look at Mhairi's features in the darkness. 'Do you believe in it?' he asked her after a few moments. 'The *Cù Sìth*? Only, you sounded like you did.'

'You think so?'

'Aye. I said it was a wolf that was attacking the sheep and you seemed to doubt that. Why?'

'Because there are no wolves. They have all been killed.'

'People say that, but it doesn't mean it's true.'

'People say there are no goblins, and it doesn't mean *that's* true either.'

'Yes, but . . . such things are just stories for children. Aren't they?'

She didn't answer that. There was another silence, then:

'Have you ever been into the Forest of Tay?' she asked him.

'No. I never heard of it until yesterday.'

'It's quite the place. You'll see.'

'What do you mean by that? Why will I see?'

'Well, you'll have to go after the creature, won't you? You'll have to follow it to its lair. And that's where it lives.'

'Who says?'

'Everyone does. You know, you should take me with you when you go in there. I know that forest better than anyone. I know all the paths. After all, it's where I came from.'

He gave her an incredulous look. 'How can that be?

'It's where they found me wandering when I was wee. Andrew's told me the story so many times.'

There was a long silence, and he was aware of her breathing just a short distance away from him.

'Well, go on then,' he prompted her.

'Go on, what?'

'Tell *me* the story. I know you want to.'

'That's a bit presumptuous.' She seemed to sense his puzzlement and added. 'Andrew sends me to a school. That's where I learnt that word. It means that you presume things. Presumptuous.'

She was beginning to annoy him. 'Are you going to tell me the story or are you not?'

'All right, if that's what you want.' She arranged herself on the straw until she was sitting cross-legged in front of him. In the ensuing silence, Callum heard the sound of an owl calling somewhere off to the east. Mhairi began to talk.

'It was twelve years ago. Andrew's parents had the inn then and it had a different name, The Oak. Andrew had married Isla just four years earlier. He had always lived at The Oak, and he brought his new bride to live there and work alongside him. There was never any doubt that when Andrew's parents had passed away, the inn would go to their son and his wife. Isla loved the place. She used to tell Andrew that she couldn't imagine a better home. But the two of them had a shared sorrow. They both longed for children but for some reason, they had never been blessed with any.

The years passed and first Andrew's mother died after she took a fall, and then, just a few months later, his father. People said he died of a broken heart – that he had lost the will to carry on without his wife. They said he loved her too much. Do you suppose that's possible?'

'I wouldn't know,' murmured Callum.

'Anyway, Andrew and Isla worked hard at the inn. They added more rooms to it and invested money making it a fine place to stay. They renamed the place the Shepherd's Crook, because Andrew thought they were like two shepherds looking after a flock of guests.

People came from all over Scotland to stay at their inn, and they prospered. And yet, they still didn't have the thing they really wanted more than anything else in the world.'

'A child,' murmured Callum.

'Aye – a wee son or daughter to call their own. And then, one night in the inn an old man told them about the Clootie Well. He said that if a person went there and made a wish—'

'Wait,' said Callum. 'What's a . . . Clootie Well?'

'You don't know?'

'I do not.'

'Well, it's . . .' Mhairi stopped talking. 'No, never mind. I'll show you, the first chance we get.'

'But I—'

'Stop interrupting! You want to hear this story or not?'

Callum sighed. 'All right, then. Carry on.'

Mhairi drew in a breath and continued. 'So, Andrew and Isla gathered together the things they needed and they rode out to the Forest of Tay. They tethered their horses on the outskirts and walked along the track that led to the well. The old man Andrew had spoken to at the inn had told him which path to take. They walked deep into the forest and finally they saw the Clootie Well ahead of them.'

'There you go again! What is a —'

'Shush! You'll find out soon enough. Don't worry, it's a good thing, you'll see! Anyway, Andrew and Isla approached the well and took out the offerings they had brought with them. They tied them in position and they made their wish – that they would be blessed with a child. And when they had done that, they started walking back to where they had left the horses, thinking that now they would just have to go home and wait to see what happened. Well, they had only gone a short distance, when they stopped in their tracks because they had heard something.'

'What?' murmured Callum, caught up in the story now.

'It was the sound of music playing.'

'Music?'

'Aye. Music such as they had never heard before – strange, lamenting, mournful music. And they stopped to listen for a while until gradually, it faded away. "That was strange," said Andrew. And then they heard another sound. Somebody was coming towards them through the trees, snapping twigs, pushing aside the bushes . . .'

'So, they ran, right?'

'Whisht, no! They did not run. What kind of an ending would that be? No, they turned to look in the direction the sounds were coming from, and what do you think they saw?'

'Umm . . . I really don't know.'

'Have a guess!'

'No, I really don't—'

'They saw me, of course!'

'You?'

'Aye, me. I was walking towards them, clad all in rags – just like the ones they had left as an offering. I was only a babe in arms, barely able to walk, but Andrew says I came striding through the bushes as though I owned the forest, as though I hadn't a care in the world. He says as I approached them, I held out my plump wee arms as though begging them to take me with them!'

'But . . . I'm sorry, but what if you were with somebody else and you just . . . wandered off?'

'Oh, no, they had a good look around, before they left. There was nobody else there, not a living soul. They took me back to the inn and they even made enquiries, asked if anybody had lost a wee bairn, but nobody ever came forward. Weeks passed and they decided that I must be a gift from the people of the woods.'

'No, wait.' Callum shook his head. 'That can't be right. Andrew doesn't believe in them! He told us that.'

Mhairi gave a low chuckle. 'He told you what you wanted to hear. But how could he not believe after they had given him such a gift? They named me Mhairi, which means 'beloved', and they raised me as their own. But as I grew up, I found myself drawn to the forest. I would beg my parents to take me there and, when I was older, I spent time there alone whenever I could. I learnt all the trails, all the paths.'

'And did you ever . . . see anything strange in there?'

'Not strange. Beautiful. I saw wonders. I came to understand that the way we live now – with our houses and our work and our precious coins – that's not how we were meant to be. Because, you see, we are just babes ourselves, only in this world for a few score years. But the forest has been there since the beginning of time. And when we are long turned to dust, it will still be there. Watching.'

Callum swallowed hard. He had already been apprehensive about going into the woods, but now he felt doubly so.

'Oh, don't worry,' murmured Mhairi, as though she knew exactly what was in his head. 'I'll take care of you in there. There's no need to be afraid.'

'I'm not afraid,' he said, a little too quickly.

'Aye,' she said. 'Of course not.' She chuckled. 'You men. You never can tell the truth about your feelings.'

Somewhere, far off, a deep voice – Andrew's voice, Callum decided – called Mhairi's name.

'I'm needed,' she said. 'I'll be off and let you get comfortable.'

'Wait,' he said.

'Umm?'

'You said you'd show me this . . . clootie thing?'

'Don't worry, I will. First chance I get. You just listen out for the supper gong. That mutton pie is good. I made it myself.'

'You're the cook as well?'

'No, Mrs Blantyre is the cook, but I help her out with some things. And everybody says my mutton pie is the best in Scotland.'

And then she was scrambling past him, jumping confidently down the ladder as though she could see perfectly in the gloom. He heard the sound of her feet thudding on to the ground and hurrying away through the open doors of the stable and across the courtyard. He sat where he was, wishing he could see better, but he could still only make out dim details. He put a hand down in the straw and winced as something dug into the flesh, something small and hard. He picked it up and lifted it to his gaze, then held it out towards the open hatch, allowing the light to illuminate it.

He was holding a little tin soldier. He was wearing a bright red tunic and had a musket slung over one shoulder. Callum strained his eyes to see better and was finally able to make out the friendly smile on the soldier's painted face. He smiled back and slipped it into his pocket, telling himself he'd hand it back to Mhairi the next time he saw her. He wasn't sure why, but he was pretty sure it belonged to her.

Then he lay down in the straw and tried to get some rest.

# 7

# OMENS

'Are you sure this is a good idea?' murmured Callum.

He was nervously following Fraser along a narrow track, between ranks of tightly packed trees. Thin shafts of moonlight occasionally managed to pierce the canopy of foliage overhead, dappling the path with restless ripples of cold white, but aside from that it was hard to see very far in any direction. Mhairi's words kept repeating themselves, over and over, in Callum 's head.

*You'll have to follow the beast to its lair . . .*

But this felt like madness. What was Fraser thinking? Surely it made more sense to lure the creature out into the open, where it could be more easily fixed in the sights of a rifle?

Fraser's gaze was intent on the way ahead. His flintlock was held ready to be snapped up into a firing position and he was placing his heavily booted feet with exaggerated care, trying to move as quietly as he could through the tangle of undergrowth.

Callum decided that his question hadn't been heard so he tried again.

'I said, are you sure—'

'Whisht, lad!' Fraser threw an angry glare over his shoulder.

'Can't you keep your trap shut for one moment? I think we're close now. Listen! Can you hear something?'

Callum stopped in his tracks and concentrated. At first, all he could make out was the soft rustling of leaves on the night wind – but then he became aware of something else. It was the distant sound of music.

'What is that?' growled Fraser.

'It sounds like . . .' Callum broke off as he realised the music was growing steadily louder. Then he remembered that he'd heard the tune before: it had been sung to him earlier that same day.

*'Poor Johnny he's a-sleepin'*
*The moonlight comes a-creepin'*
*And all his children gather now*
*To sing their last goodbyes . . .'*

'That's the tune the old woman was singing,' he croaked.

'What old woman?'

'The one who was washing her clothes in the stream. There was . . . blood on those clothes.'

'So? What better reason to wash them?'

'But you didn't see how much of it there was. The whole river . . .'

'Can't you be quiet?' snapped Fraser. 'I'm trying to . . . oh! Listen now.' He pointed away to his right. 'What's *that*?'

Another sound was replacing the music. Something was approaching through the undergrowth to their left – pushing aside bushes, snapping dry twigs underfoot. Fraser swung his rifle up to his eyeline and turned his gaze towards the noisy approach.

'The wolf's coming,' he said. He sounded surprisingly calm.

'No,' Callum assured him. Because Mhairi's story was suddenly in his head. 'It could be a wee child coming out from the Clootie Well. Someone must have wished for one!'

'What are you babbling about? What baby makes a sound like that?'

It was a good question. Whatever was coming was accelerating now, smashing the vegetation recklessly aside as it raced towards its quarry. Judging from the noise, it was too big – and much too fast – to be human.

'B-but Mhairi said . . .'

'Shut your mouth and pass me my pistol. It may take more than one shot to finish it off!'

Callum fumbled the heavy gun from its holster and held it out. Fraser half-turned to reach for it, but the hand that emerged from the sleeve of his coat was a massive hairy paw. Callum stared open-mouthed at it for a moment, then snapped his horrified gaze upwards. The face regarding him from under Fraser's wide brimmed hat was no longer that of a man.

It had a long, drooling snout and eyes that blazed like red hot coals . . .

\*\*\*

Callum opened his eyes and sat up with a gasp of terror. He stayed where he was for a moment, sitting in the half-light, the sounds of the dinner gong still reverberating in his head. His heart was thudding in his chest like a military drum. He looked blearily around and realised what had happened. Tired from the long ride here, he had fallen asleep in the hay loft.

'Supper!' he heard a female voice yell and remembered how hungry he was. Yet, as he clambered clumsily down the ladder, he couldn't rid himself of the last image from that awful dream – Fraser's jaws hinging open to reveal rows of dripping yellow fangs.

Callum stepped down on to solid ground and turned away from the ladder, only to have his heart lurch in his chest a second time. The old ostler, Tam, was standing inches away from him, as though he'd been waiting for him to descend.

'You made me jump!' complained Callum.

Tam didn't seem to care about that. He leant closer, his grizzled features set in a furious scowl. Callum was aware of the rank smell of him, a heady mixture of tobacco smoke and pork fat. 'Don't ye be talking to that wee shargie,' he growled.

Callum frowned. 'Why not?' he muttered. 'She seems friendly.'

Tam shook his head. 'Nah,' he said. 'Dinna be fooled by her. She's a shargie. And ye canna trust them.'

The gong sounded again from the direction of the inn.

'I'm away for my supper,' announced Callum, stepping around the old man. He hurried towards the open doors of the stable.

'Aye, go and eat,' growled Tam. 'While ye still can.'

Callum wasn't sure what that meant, but he didn't intend to stand around discussing the matter. He strode across the cobbled yard and in through the front door of the Shepherd's Crook, where he found Fraser sitting at the same table they'd both occupied earlier. There were a couple of men standing at the bar, holding tankards of ale and talking to Fraser. From the expression on his face, it was clear he wasn't enjoying the conversation. On the other side of the counter, Andrew watched the three of them sternly. Other people, presumably guests at the inn, sat quietly in the corners, supping their drinks.

'. . . and what do you suppose *you'll* be able to do that Hamish could'nae?' the taller of the two men was asking Fraser. He was a bald, gangling sort of fellow with a prominent, beak-like nose.

'Aye,' said his companion, a tubby man with a thatch of ginger hair and a selection of crooked tobacco-stained teeth. 'Gilmour was a brave soul and the best shot in these parts, everybody said so.'

Fraser looked unimpressed. 'With respect, gentlemen, Mr Gilmour was a shepherd. I, on the other hand, was a professional soldier for fifteen years. I've seen so-called brave men turn and run when confronted with something they have no experience of. Gilmour may have been a decent shot, but I have killed men and animals alike – plenty of them. To me, that's all in a day's work.' He looked up as Callum approached. 'Ah, here's my assistant,' he said. 'Come and sit, lad. I'm told that our food will arrive presently.'

Callum did as he was told. The two customers studied him for a moment. They seemed amused.

'He doesn't look much of a wolf hunter,' said the bald man. 'How old is he, anyway? Twelve?'

'I'm fourteen,' said Callum. 'Nearly fifteen.'

'Oh, a fearless age,' said the ginger man. 'I dimly remember my own youth. I went wherever I liked, did whatever occurred to me. Happy days. And how many men have you killed, may I ask?'

'I beg your pardon?' said Callum.

Fraser gave one of his mirthless laughs. 'The boy is merely here to fetch and carry for me,' he said. 'Of course, I wouldn't entrust such duties to one of his tender years.'

The bald man sniggered. 'You could always send him on ahead of you,' he suggested. 'Use him as wolf bait.'

'If you believe it *is* a wolf,' said his companion quietly.

Fraser fixed the man with a cold stare. 'What else could it be?' he asked. 'Don't tell me you're one of those who believes I'm going after some kind of demon creature.'

The ginger man gazed back, untroubled. 'Where is Hamish Gilmour, then?' he asked. 'If he'd been killed by a wolf there'd be some remains left out on the moors, wouldn't there? But not a trace of him has been found. Not so much as a finger bone.'

'*Yet*,' added Fraser. 'But then you've not had an expert tracker on the case, have you? Until now.'

Callum looked at Fraser suspiciously. This was the first time he'd heard any mention of that particular skill.

'And where did you learn to track?' asked the bald man.

'In the army,' said Fraser. 'When the quarry was a good deal deadlier than some four-legged miscreant.'

At that moment, Mhairi came into the room carrying a heavily laden tray. 'Good evening, gentlemen,' she said. 'Here is your supper. I hope you've good appetites.' She put the tray down and placed a bowl and a spoon in front of each of the diners. The bowls contained a steaming hunk of pie, dark gravy leaking out from under a golden-brown crust. Callum leant forward and inhaled the rich, meaty aroma.

'Smells good,' he said enthusiastically.

'Tastes even better,' Mhairi assured him. 'Like I said, I made it myself. It'll put hairs on your chest.' She went to the bar and picked up the two tankards of ale that Andrew had just dispensed. She brought them to the table.

'Have a care, gentlemen,' warned the ginger man, who was still observing the diners. 'Nobody knows what ingredients Mhairi puts into those pies. We've asked her many times, but she won't give up her secrets. Even Mrs Blantyre claims not to know the recipe.'

'It's just a secret blend of herbs and spices,' said Mhairi. 'Handed down over the years.'

'Aye, but handed down by whom?' asked the bald man.

'That's enough now,' said Andrew, giving the two men a certain look. 'Why don't we let our guests eat their supper in peace, eh? There's plenty of space in the back room. I'll bring more drinks through to you.' They looked reluctant to leave until he added, 'On the house,' at which point they turned happily aside and headed for a doorway in the back wall.

'Good hunting,' the bald man called over his shoulder.

'Keep your eyes peeled,' added the ginger man. 'And your powder dry.'

Fraser threw a disparaging look after them. 'Wherever you go, it's the same story,' he muttered. 'People who think they know better than you.'

'Ah, pay them no heed, sir,' said Mhairi. 'Those two are well known for their ability to talk and not much else.' She looked at Callum, who was already tucking into his bowl of food. 'How's that pie?' she asked him.

His mouth was too full to make much of a reply, but he nodded eagerly and held up a thumb. He wanted to tell her that it was around a hundred times tastier than Mother McCloud's dismal attempts at cooking, but couldn't say that in front of his employer. Fraser picked up a spoon and began to eat his own portion, but the look on his face gave no indication of whether or not he liked what he was tasting. He seemed to remember something.

'You haven't seen my best shirt, have you?' he murmured.

'Your shirt?'

'Aye, the white one. I definitely told Mother McCloud to put it in my pack, but there's no sign of it.'

Callum shook his head. He was about to say something, but Andrew leant his elbows on the bar and gave them an enquiring look.

'May I ask about your plans for tomorrow?' he said.

Fraser chewed a mouthful of food before replying. 'We'll rise at first light,' he said. 'I'd like to begin by having a look at the site of the alleged attack. I suppose you can supply me with directions?'

Andrew smiled. 'I can do better than that. Mhairi can take you there.'

'Mhairi?' Fraser looked at the girl doubtfully. 'I'm not sure that's a suitable task for a girl,' he said. 'It could be dangerous.' He looked at her. 'Can you even ride a horse?' he asked her.

'Probably better than you,' she told him, and received a warning glare from Andrew.

'Now, now, Mhairi, let's remember our manners in front of guests.'

'Sorry, Andrew.' Callum noticed that she didn't call him 'father'.

'Oh, that's all right,' said Fraser, waving his spoon. 'I admire frankness.'

'Mhairi is an accomplished horsewoman,' Andrew assured him. 'And she knows the locality well. Furthermore, Mr McCloud, if your enquiries are likely to take you into the Forest of Tay at any time, you really should consider letting her be your guide. She knows that place better than anyone.'

Fraser seemed amused by this claim. 'And how is that possible?' he asked. Again, he studied Mhairi. 'You have spent time there?'

'Every spare minute,' she assured him. 'I know it as I know the back of my hand, sir.'

'Well, let's first see if you can manage to guide us to the place where Hamish Gilmour was attacked. You'll need to be ready at sun-up, mind.'

'Not a problem, sir.'

'And there'll be no mollycoddling, either. If you can't keep up, you'll be left behind.'

Callum stopped eating for a moment and looked at his employer, uncertainly.

'But . . . if she's leading us there, then how . . .?'

'Just eat your supper,' growled Fraser.

Callum put his head down and went back to his meal. Mhairi picked up the tray and turned to leave, but as she did so, she directed a sly wink at Callum. She went out of the room and Callum stared thoughtfully after her.

'She's a strange one,' observed Fraser, loud enough for Andrew to hear. 'She has all the confidence of a boy.'

'And many of the skills,' added Andrew. 'She's always been a puzzle, though. I think she takes after her mother, more than she does, me.'

Callum looked at the landlord blankly. If Mhairi had been telling the truth about her mysterious discovery in the Forest of Tay, then Andrew surely wasn't referring to his own late wife, Isla. Who then did he think Mhairi's true mother was?

'But, I thought Mhairi was . . . adopted,' said Callum quietly.

'Did she tell you that?' Andrew looked amused. 'Ah, you shouldn't believe everything that comes out of her mouth, lad. That one's away with the fairies.' He chuckled. 'But rest assured, gentlemen. She'll take you where you need to go tomorrow. Of that you can be sure.'

# 8

# HUNTER'S MOON

Once back in the hayloft, Callum drifted off into a deep sleep and this time there were no bad dreams to trouble him. But, after what seemed like only a few moments, a hand was on his shoulder, shaking him roughly awake. He lay there, startled, and could just discern a face peering down into his. He was aware of Mhairi's fragrant smell, a mingling of peppermint and lavender.

'Wh-what's wrong?' he gasped.

'Nothing. I came to fetch you. I have your horse saddled below.'

He blinked. 'My horse?'

'Aye. You wanted to see the Clootie Well, didn't you?'

He lay there staring up at her. 'What, *now*?' he hissed. 'What time is it?'

'Time to go and see it, of course. Come on, lazy bones, stir yourself.' And before he could question her again, she had moved to the hatch and was clambering nimbly down the ladder. Callum shook the last dregs of sleep out of his head and followed her. He went down the rungs to the ground and saw that, sure enough, Molly was saddled and ready to go. Beside her stood a tall, white stallion, a beautiful-looking creature with wild eyes and flared nostrils. Mhairi was standing a short distance away looking down at the prostrate figure of old Tam, who was lying on his back on a pile of straw – his toothless mouth open, his eyes closed. Beside him, an overturned clay beaker trailed a splash of dark red liquid.

Callum came to stand beside Mhairi. 'What's wrong with him?' he murmured. 'He looks dead to the world.'

'He's just asleep,' she said. 'Don't worry, he won't wake till long after we're home.' She prodded the beaker with the toe of her boot.

'You ... didn't give him something, did you?' whispered Callum.

She turned to him, all wide-eyed innocence. 'What makes you think I'd do a thing like that?' she said, and gave him the weirdest smile. 'Come on,' she said. 'We've a way to go. Don't mount up until we're clear of the courtyard.'

They led their horses out of the stable and quietly across the cobbles. Once out on to open ground, Mhairi swung herself lithely up into the saddle. Callum followed in a more clumsy fashion.

'Where did you get that horse?' he murmured. 'He's a beauty.'

'His name is Blizzard,' she said. 'He was a gift from an admirer. I think someone was trying to impress me.'

Callum didn't know what to say to that but luckily, Mhairi drummed her heels into the stallion's flanks and took off at full gallop. After a moment's hesitation, Callum followed.

*Where is she taking me?*

The thought flashed briefly through his mind, but it required all his effort to keep up with her, as the white horse raced like a phantom across the moonlit landscape.

\*\*\*

They rode hell for leather for around half an hour, then finally crested a ridge where Mhairi brought Blizzard to a halt. On a stretch of plain below them, Callum could see the edge of the forest cutting like a black swathe across the horizon. He was vividly reminded of the dream he'd had just before Colonel Chivers arrived, but as far as he could see, there were no lights emanating from these woods. Closer than that, he could also see areas where the jagged stumps of many trees stuck up from bare earth, revealing that the land had recently been cleared. Mhairi urged her horse on again at a more leisurely pace, descending the slope and moving out across the ravaged ground, looking sternly around as she led the way.

'Is this the land that Colonel Chivers cleared?' asked Callum.

'Aye,' said Mhairi. 'It seems that all the acres that already surround his home were not enough for him. He decided to build a hunting lodge for all his fine friends to visit so they could wander into the outskirts of the forest and shoot at whatever they liked.' She shook her head. 'He was warned not to clear this part of the forest.'

'Who warned him?' asked Callum.

'Several people on the estate. But he didn't listen.' She pointed to something they were approaching; a raised area of ground, perhaps some twenty feet across, that was marked out by a circle of boulders that had been arranged into a huge spiral – the largest stones around the outside, growing progressively smaller as they moved inwards towards the spiral's centre. 'He was told that if he cut down the trees that enclosed that circle, he would pay a terrible price.'

Callum gazed down at it, puzzled. 'What is it?' he asked.

'It's a faerie ring, of course. Have you never seen one before?'

He shook his head. 'Never,' he admitted. 'What is it, exactly?'

'It's a sacred shrine built by the people of the forest,'

said Mhairi. 'It's where they used to hold their ceremonies, back in the time when the whole of this area belonged to them. But Chivers' workmen came here and cut down all the trees that hid it from the world. The colonel had to pay a pretty penny to persuade the locals to do it. He even had to bring some people in from outside the area.'

'Like he brought in Fraser?'

She didn't answer that, and they rode slowly past the stones.

Callum remembered something else and reached into his pocket. 'I found this in the hayloft,' he said. 'I thought it might belong to you.' He showed her the lead soldier.

'Ah,' she said, smiling. 'Wee Davie. I wondered what happened to him.'

'Wee Davie?' he echoed.

'Oh, when I was little, I used to set him to guard me when I was sleeping. I had quite a few of these soldiers, a whole battalion of them. I think they belonged to Andrew when he was a boy and I . . . borrowed them.' She slipped the lead figure into the pocket of her dress. 'Thank you for returning him,' she said. 'I've missed him.'

'You're welcome,' said Callum. He studied her for a moment. 'You really believe in these walkers in the woods?' he asked. 'I mean, isn't it all a bit . . .?'

'A bit what?'

'Fanciful?'

She didn't reply to that question either. They rode on in silence until they had crossed the cleared land and reached the outskirts of the forest. There, Mhairi dismounted and tied Blizzard's reins to the branch of a tree. Callum followed suit with Molly and stood, gazing apprehensively into the thick undergrowth. 'We're really going in there?' he murmured. 'In the dark? Shouldn't we have brought a lantern with us?'

Mhairi smiled. 'There's no need,' she said, looking upwards. 'We have a hunter's moon to light our way.'

He raised his own gaze heavenwards and for the first time noticed how full the moon was – and the strange red caste that coloured it. For some reason, the image filled him with dread. He couldn't help thinking about the washerwoman at the ford, the twisting trails of blood spilling from the shirt she held in her webbed fingers. He turned to look back at Mhairi, meaning to ask her why it was called a hunter's moon, but she was already walking into the trees, following a path that he hadn't even been aware of. She paused and looked back at him. 'Are ye coming or not?' she asked him.

He nodded and fell obediently into step behind her. In a matter of moments, the forest closed around them as though swallowing them whole.

\*\*\*

They walked for what seemed like hours, heading deeper and deeper into the undergrowth, but Mhairi seemed to know exactly where she was going, stooping occasionally to avoid low-hanging branches, using her arms to push aside thick fronds of vegetation. Callum marvelled at her natural grace as he stumbled clumsily along in her wake, his clothing snagging on unseen twigs, his feet tripping on hidden roots. Every so often, sounds rang through the forest; the shrill cries of birds, the barking of foxes and other chittering noises that he couldn't identify. He felt as though he was slowly drowning in a bowl of dank green soup.

At last, he heard Mhairi mutter, 'Here we are,' and he leant sideways to peer past her. There was a clearing ahead of them and he felt a chill go through him as he registered a weird, green glow emanating from a series of strange shapes dotted around a pool of water, tall multi-coloured things he couldn't quite make out. Again, he was reminded of his dream. Mhairi led him closer and only then did he recognise the glowing shapes for what they were. They were just trees, but they had clumps of brightly coloured rags tied to their branches, so many of them that the lower limbs were completely covered in fabric. What's more, it was the rags that were glowing with that green light.

'What is that?' whispered Callum fearfully.

They walked nearer still, until they were close enough for Callum to study one of the trees in more detail. He drew in a sharp breath. He could see now that the bits of fabric were liberally coated with a multitude of small striped insects, each one of which had a glowing green tail.

'Fireflies,' he murmured. 'But I've never seen so many.' He reached out to touch a scrap of red rag and a cluster of insects fluttered into the air and buzzed around his head before settling themselves on a new perch. Mhairi leant close to study them and her face was weirdly illuminated by the glow. She smiled and the light was reflected in her eyes, giving them an unsettling gleam.

'These are the females,' she whispered. 'They make that light to attract males. It's late in the year for this, but everything has been disrupted by the clearing of the land.'

'And the bits of cloth?' Callum leant in closer. Four words had been inked on to the strip he was looking at and he could just make them out. *Cure me of gout.* He frowned, focusing on another. *I am lame. Help me walk.* And then, one more. *Please give us a child.*

'People come here to ask for help,' explained Mhairi. 'All the time.' She pointed to the pool of water. 'Sometimes they wash their afflicted parts in the enchanted water. Others throw coins in there and speak their wish aloud.' She noticed how Callum's eyes moved with interest to the pool and added, 'It's the worst luck ever to take money from the pool.'

'Oh, I wasn't going to,' he said, but couldn't be sure she was convinced.

'People have been coming here and making wishes for generations,' said Mhairi.

'And it works?'

'I'm the proof of that,' she said.

Callum frowned. 'Andrew said . . .' He trailed off, wary of saying what was on his mind.

'Go on,' she said. 'Speak up.'

'He said that I was not to believe everything you told me. He said you were . . . away with the fairies.'

She tilted back her head and laughed. 'Yes, well, he would say that, wouldn't he?' She gave Callum a scornful look. 'You must understand, Callum, Andrew is a decent man, but he became a wealthy landlord by changing his story, depending on who he was talking to.'

'But he said that you take after your mother. Meaning, I think, his late wife. Only you told me—'

'Isla Sessions was not my mother,' she assured him. 'And Andrew has no idea who was. Nobody knows, including me.' She stepped away from the tree and moved closer to the pool of water. 'While we're here,' she said, 'you might want to make a wish yourself.'

He frowned. 'What would I wish for?' he asked her.

'Oh, I don't know. Perhaps a father who is a better card player?'

He glared at her. 'How do you know about that?' he asked her. 'Have you been talking to Fraser?'

She laughed. 'No, I haven't. Perhaps you were talking in your sleep when I came to wake you.'

'Was I?'

'Maybe.'

He made a valiant attempt to change the subject. 'So, this beast we're after. Do you believe it's a wolf or a *coo shee* thing?'

'It's no wolf,' she assured him. 'And it's *Cù Sìth*.'

'So, what exactly is that?'

'An ancient creature, summoned from the underworld by the walkers in the woods and sent out to avenge them.'

Callum shook his head. 'But that doesn't make sense. Hamish Gilmour was just a shepherd.'

'He was also handy with an axe, by all accounts. And the farming has been hard this year. When somebody offers you handsome money to help clear some forest, it's hard to resist.'

Callum gasped. 'You're saying that Hamish . . .'

'. . . took money from Colonel Chivers. Yes. And has it not occurred to Mr McCloud to ask about the *other* victims?'

Only then did Callum remember that meeting they'd had with the colonel. He had said that others had been attacked – but at the time, he and Fraser had both supposed the old man had been talking about sheep.

'You're saying other *people* have gone missing?' he cried.

'Aye. Three other men, all with but one thing in common.'

'They . . . oh, you mean . . . they helped to cut down the trees?'

She grinned. 'Now you're catching on. You might want to ask Colonel Chivers about it the next time you see him.' She gestured at the pool of water. 'Last chance to make a wish,' she told him. 'We need to be going soon.'

He looked at her for a moment and even opened his mouth to say he didn't believe in such nonsense, but then he was scrambling impulsively closer to the water and kneeling on the bank. He reached into his pocket and found the only thing of value that he had – a single coin that he'd been saving for an emergency. He reached out and let it drop into the water, then whispered under his breath, 'Please let me come through this alive.'

He gazed into the clear water and realised with a shock that the bottom of the shallow pool was literally covered with a glittering layer of assorted coins. He stared at them for a moment and then lifted his head at the sound of an owl hooting somewhere away in the distance. He got back to his feet and saw that Mhairi was already retracing her steps along the track that had brought them here. He hurried after her.

'I'm thinking,' he said. 'What about Fraser?'

She glanced at him. 'What about him?'

'He's taken money from the colonel to hunt the creature. Hey, you don't think . . .?'

'I think he should be careful who he does business with,' said Mhairi. She sighed. 'But I know it isn't easy. There are so many here in the same boat. Just struggling to make ends meet. Andrew is putting you and Fraser up at the inn. You don't suppose he's doing that out of the goodness of his heart, do you? Of course, the colonel is paying him for the room and the meals.'

'But neither he nor Fraser chopped down any trees!'

'True. I'm just not sure the *Cù Sìth* is the kind of creature that is willing to make exceptions. If I were you, I'd try and persuade Fraser to give that money back. If only for your own sake.'

Callum frowned. 'For *my* sake?'

'Aye. Well, if some of that money is coming to you . . .'

He laughed bitterly at that. 'Chance would be a fine thing! Fraser doesn't pay me for my work, if that's what you're thinking.'

She gave him a puzzled look. 'Then why are you with him?'

'It's complicated,' he told her. 'But take it from me, there's no way on earth I'll be able to persuade Fraser to hand back his fee. That man lives for making money.'

He was going to say something else but then he heard a sound – a long, drawn-out howl that seemed to echo throughout the entire forest. He looked at Mhairi, wide-eyed. 'Is that . . . is that the *Cù Sìth?*' he whispered. 'It sounds very close.'

She shrugged. 'Perhaps. But we have nothing to worry about. I have never taken a penny from Colonel Chivers and, from what you've just told me, you're safe too. And besides, you just made a wish, didn't you? And, no offence, but I've a pretty good idea what you asked for.'

And with that, she strolled on along the trail as if she hadn't a single care in the world.

# 9

# VISITORS

Callum climbed back into the hayloft and was so exhausted, his eyes closed the moment he stretched himself out on the soft straw. He slept deeply and, after what seemed like only moments, was jolted awake by the harsh sound of Fraser's urgent voice calling from below.

'Callum! Get yourself down here, you lazy good-for-nothing. The sun's up and we're ready to go!'

Callum blinked furiously until his vision swam into focus. He yawned, then dragged himself over to the ladder and half-climbed, half-fell down the rungs, until his boots clumped on the stable floor. Old Tam was sitting on his straw mattress, yawning and stretching as though unwilling to stir his ancient bones into motion. The dazed look in the old man's eyes convinced Callum that Mhairi really had put some powerful sleeping draught into the old man's wine last night.

'What are you staring at?' muttered Tam.

'Nothing much,' said Callum and trudged past him, out through the open stable doors, to find that the world was enveloped in a thick, grey mist. Fraser and Mhairi were waiting for him, looking like two phantoms sitting astride their horses.

Mhairi was holding Molly by the reins and smiling down at him.

'Morning, sleepyhead,' she greeted him.

'This girl puts us all to shame,' observed Fraser. 'She had the horses saddled up and ready before that so-called ostler had managed to move so much as a muscle. You need to take a leaf out of her book, boy.'

Mhairi leant over in the saddle as she handed Callum his reins and gave him a grin. 'Praise indeed,' she murmured.

'Aren't you tired?' he asked her incredulously.

By way of answer, she pressed a warm, cloth-wrapped package into his hand. 'A wee bit of breakfast for you,' she murmured, then sat upright again. She glanced back at Fraser. 'If you'll just follow me, Mr McCloud,' she suggested and kicked her heels into Blizzard's flanks. The white horse moved away at speed and Fraser spurred his own mount into motion. Callum clambered awkwardly into his saddle and paused a moment to investigate the warm parcel. He found it contained a hunk of freshly baked soda bread and he gratefully took a mouthful from it, before heading after the fast-disappearing shapes of his companions.

In the mist, the moor was eerily silent, the thudding of hooves curiously muffled. Callum got Molly up to a gallop, not wanting the others to get too far ahead of him, knowing it would be all too easy to lose sight of them in this.

They rode in silence for quite some time, Callum taking surreptitious bites from the bread, knowing that if Fraser saw him eating, he'd make a point of complaining about it. As ever, Mhairi appeared to know exactly where she was going, never slowing her pace for a moment. As Callum finally came alongside Fraser, he heard his employer mutter grudgingly, 'That one rides as well as any man.'

'Better than most,' said Callum.

Fraser gave him a critical look. 'Don't you be getting too chummy with her,' he said. 'You *do* know what people around here say about her?'

'I do,' said Callum. 'But you don't believe them, do you?'

'Of course not,' said Fraser. But for once, Callum thought, his voice lacked its usual authority.

They galloped onwards, into the mist.

*\*\*\**

By the time they reached the bothy, the sun was beginning to break through the grey blanket of mist and visibility was rapidly improving. Mhairi brought Blizzard to a halt a short distance from the hut and waited for the others to catch up with her. She pointed to the bothy.

'This is where Hamish waited for the creature,' she said. She twisted in her saddle. 'The dead ram was lying over yonder.'

Fraser dismounted and walked to the bothy. He pushed open the ramshackle door with his boot, peered cautiously into the interior, then went inside. The door swung shut.

'He's wasting his time,' said Mhairi. 'We already had a good look around in there.' She smiled at Callum. 'Did you enjoy the bread?' she asked him.

'I did. When did you find time to make that?'

'First thing this morning,' she assured him. 'I had an hour to spare.'

'Do you ever sleep?' he asked her, but before she could answer, the door of the bothy opened and Fraser came out, shaking his head. 'Nothing,' he said. 'The place is as bare as a pauper's pantry. Let's see if we can find any traces of that ram.' He took Mags's reins and started to walk her towards the ridge. Callum and Mhairi rode alongside him, until they had crested the rise and were looking down into the declivity beyond. After a few moments, Callum caught sight of a flash of white amidst the bracken.

'There's something,' he said, pointing. He dismounted and handed his reins to Mhairi, then followed Fraser down the hill to inspect what he'd seen. It was a ram's skull, sure enough, stripped clean of flesh, its curved horns glinting in the rising sunlight. Fraser prodded it with the toe of one boot.

'Is this all that's left of it?' he muttered incredulously. He looked around, but there was nothing else to be seen. 'That's odd,' he muttered. 'No bloodstains, no wool, no shards of bone. Our wolf must be the daintiest eater on God's earth.' He gestured helplessly around. 'How am I expected to pick up a trail from this?'

Callum didn't have an answer for him. He could only stand, staring down at the skull. Its jagged teeth appeared to be grinning mirthlessly up at him.

'Somebody's coming,' called Mhairi, and Fraser and Callum lifted their heads to look in the direction she was pointing. Sure enough, a horseman was approaching from the west, riding fast – a tall man in a long, grey overcoat. As he came nearer, Callum recognised him. It was Michael, the coach driver who had brought Colonel Chivers to Fraser's house, but this morning he had opted to ride a bay mare, which he looked somehow much too big for.

Fraser and Callum climbed back to the top of the ridge to meet him. He reined his horse in and stared down at them gravely.

'Colonel Chivers sent me to find you,' he said. 'I tried the inn, but they told me you were headed over here.'

'Something wrong?' asked Fraser.

Michael frowned. 'I'm to take you to the Gilmour croft,' he said. 'Straight away. There's been an incident.'

'What kind of incident?' asked Callum, but Michael ignored him and kept his gaze fixed on Fraser.

'We should waste no more time,' he said, and wheeled his horse around. 'Follow me.' Then he spurred his horse back into motion.

Fraser glared after him for a moment. 'What's the matter with people around here?' he complained. 'Nobody seems to want to tell you anything.'

But he climbed obediently back into his saddle and gestured to Callum to do the same.

'Shall I come along?' asked Mhairi, and Fraser nodded.

In moments, the three of them were on their way again, following the groom's distant figure.

***

As they approached the croft, they could all see that something was badly wrong. Even at a distance, it was evident that the building's stout wooden door had been smashed asunder and now just a few scraps of splintered wood hung from its twisted hinges.

It was then that Callum remembered something that Mrs Gilmour had said when he and Fraser were last here. A sour feeling rose in his gut.

'What the hell happened to that door?' muttered Fraser. 'Looks like somebody took a battering ram to it.' He turned to look at Michael and saw that the coachman had already dropped back and was slowing his mount to a halt. 'Aren't you coming in with us?' Fraser shouted to him, but Michael shook his head.

'I have urgent business elsewhere,' he said. He tried to keep his face expressionless, but it was evident to Callum that he was scared of entering the building. He turned his horse around.

'But hang on a moment, man, you can't just . . .'

Fraser broke off as Michael galloped away. He muttered something under his breath and continued on towards the croft. He reined Mags to a halt a short distance from the building and his companions followed suit. They all sat for a moment, staring uneasily at the croft.

'I don't like this,' whispered Callum to Mhairi. 'Mrs Gilmour told us something yesterday.'

'Oh, what was that?'

'She said that she took money from Colonel Chivers.'

Mhairi raised her eyebrows. 'Really?'

'Aye. She didn't want to, but she needed money to feed her bairns and thought she had no other choice.'

Mhairi frowned. 'That's not good news,' she said.

Fraser dismounted. He pulled his flintlock from its carrier, swung the weapon into his arms and started moving slowly towards the doorway, then gestured impatiently for Callum to back him up. Callum swallowed hard. He glanced apprehensively at Mhairi for a moment, then climbed down from his mount and collected Fraser's pistol from its holder. He followed, trying to place his feet as carefully as possible. He saw Fraser's body tense as a sound came from within the building, a sudden rattling noise, as though something had just been knocked over. There were other sounds of movement within. A rustling, followed by a dull thud. Fraser lifted the flintlock up to his eyeline and cocked the trigger. He drew in a breath and stepped decisively through the open doorway. Callum steeled himself for the sound of a gunshot, but instead, heard Fraser's voice bark a terse command.

'Put your hands up where I can see them!'

Puzzled, Callum leant cautiously around the doorframe and saw that Fraser had his rifle pointed at a tall, bald man, who was holding a sack in one of his upraised hands. Callum recognised him as one of the two men they'd talked to at the inn the previous night. He was glaring at Fraser in outrage.

'Lower that weapon before you kill somebody,' he snarled.

Fraser seemed to consider the instruction for a few moments before complying. He moved further into the croft, his boots crunching on shards of broken pottery and Callum went after him. He could see now that the interior of the room looked as though it had been set upon by people armed with sledgehammers. The chairs and pine table were now no more than heaps of splintered wood on the dirt floor.

'What's been going on here?' asked Fraser. 'Where's Mrs Gilmour?'

'That's a very good question.'

'And what are you doing with that sack?'

'Just collecting a few things I need,' said the bald man. 'I'm not robbing the place if that's what you're thinking.'

'Colonel Chivers sent us here,' explained Fraser. 'Said there'd been an incident.' He lowered the flintlock's stock to the floor and gazed slowly around. 'What in the name of God happened?' he wondered.

'A visitor came,' said the bald man. 'And one I suspect that God had nothing to do with.'

'I know you,' said Fraser. 'We spoke at the inn last night. But I didn't catch your name.'

'I'm Robert Gillespie, but everyone calls me Robbie. I'm the Gilmour's nearest neighbour. My croft is just over the way.' Robbie pointed towards the open door and saw that Mhairi was now making her way inside. 'Ah, I might have known you'd be here,' he said. 'Wherever there's trouble, you'll find the landlord's daughter, eh?'

'That's funny,' said Mhairi. 'I was just thinking the same about you.'

Robbie returned his gaze to Fraser. 'All I can tell you is the widow Gilmour's bairns came hammering on my door in the early hours of this morning, screaming about something happening back here. The two of them were in their nightshirts and frightened half out of their wits. They said . . .'

He broke off, so Callum prompted him. 'What did they say?'

'. . . that something had come into their croft in the middle of the night and attacked their mother. She screamed for them to go for help, even as the thing was on her. The poor wee devils took to their heels and fled.'

'Did they describe this creature to you?' asked Fraser.

Robbie shook his head. 'It was dark, they couldn't see much. But they were terrified.'

'So . . .' Fraser looked around the room. 'There's a body, is there?'

Robbie shook his head.

'Signs of an attack, then? Bloodstains, drag marks, things like that?'

'Nothing. The same as with Hamish and the others. It's as though they just vanished into thin air.'

'The *others*?' Callum saw Fraser's baffled expression and remembered that this was the first he'd heard about it. 'What others?'

'The three men who suffered the same fate. Good heavens, man, didn't the colonel bother to tell you about them?'

Fraser could only stare at Robbie in mute shock.

'Where are the children now?' asked Mhairi.

'Back at my place. My wife is trying to calm them as best she can, but they are close to hysteria. I walked over here at first light to pick up a few of their belongings, until we can work out what to do with them. As far as I know, they have no relatives around these parts. My wife said, "go and get them something to wear."' He saw Fraser's disbelieving look and opened the sack he was carrying to show it contained nothing more than bundles of clothing. 'There,' he said. 'No valuables. Do you really think I would rob from one of my own neighbours?'

'Calm down, Robbie,' Mhairi told him. 'Nobody's accusing you of anything. We're just trying to find out what happened here.'

'Another three men, you say,' croaked Fraser. 'Missing?'

'Yes. I'm surprised you didn't know about them. I think the colonel is a little too careful about what he tells people.'

Fraser turned away and started moving quietly around the room, as if searching for clues, but Callum could see he was troubled. 'I don't understand what happened to the door,' he muttered.

'What do you think happened to it?' said Robbie scornfully. 'That's how the thing got in here. Smashed its way in.'

'It would be a mighty wolf that could do that to an oak door,' said Fraser.

Robbie laughed bitterly. 'Oh, you're still clinging to that belief, are you?' he said. 'Here, let me show you something that might change your mind.' He walked to the overturned table and indicated the thick edge of its top, a place where a great ragged chunk had been torn from it. Callum felt his stomach lurch. The jagged edges of the missing section were coated with what looked like saliva. 'I suppose you'll say that no wolf could have done that,' said Robbie. 'And you'd be absolutely right. Face the truth, man. This is the work of the *Cù Sìth*.'

Fraser shook his head. 'I do not believe such nonsense,' he said. 'And I never will!'

'Suit yourself,' said Robbie. 'Some people won't believe what's right in front of their eyes. That's up to you.' He swung the sack up on to his shoulder. 'Now, if you'll excuse me, I'll head back to my croft and see about getting those poor bairns clothed and fed.' He gave Fraser a mocking look. 'The ones who have just been orphaned by something that doesn't exist.'

'You don't know for sure they are orphaned,' retorted Fraser.

'You think not? Look around you, man. Do you really think there's any chance that Shona Gilmour is going to come wandering back here alive and well?'

Fraser stared at him. 'And are you not worried about walking across the moor by yourself?' he asked. 'If this hellish beast you speak of is still at large.'

Robbie gave him a despairing look.

'I don't have a care in the world in broad daylight,' he said. 'The *Cù Sìth* only hunts in darkness. Everyone knows that.'

Callum thought about the howl he and Mhairi had heard in the deep forest in the small hours of this same morning.

He glanced at Mhairi and saw that she was thinking about it too. They all watched as Robbie went out of the door and trudged away across the moor.

There was a long silence. Fraser seemed to be in deep thought. Then he raised his head and looked at Mhairi.

'You know where the colonel lives?' he asked her.

She nodded.

'Lead us there, will you?' he said. 'I think it's time we had a long talk with Colonel Chivers.'

# 10

# CHIVERS HALL

They rode in silence, Fraser and Callum following Mhairi, who seemed far from thrilled at the prospect of visiting the colonel's home. Her face had been set in a scowl ever since she left the Gilmours' croft. At one point, she led them past the land that had recently been cleared, the stumps of felled trees looking even more shocking in broad daylight than they had the previous night. Callum wondered if Mhairi had deliberately brought them this way as a reminder of what the estate owner had been responsible for. Fraser looked with interest at the big spiral of stones in the midst of the sea of stumps. Deciding he'd had enough silence for one day, Callum leant over in his saddle and told him, 'That's the faerie circle you're looking at.'

Fraser studied him contemptuously for a moment. 'Is it indeed?' he muttered. 'This is where they dance about in the middle of the night, I suppose, casting their spells and singing their magical songs?' He nodded towards Mhairi. 'And she told you all about it, did she?'

Callum found the nerve to gaze back at his employer. 'What if she did? She's not alone. It's what lots of people around here believe.'

Fraser leant over in his saddle and spat, signalling that as far as he was concerned, the conversation was over.

Chivers Hall was in sight for a long time before they finally came to its magnificent stone gateway. The metal barred gates were closed and guarded by a couple of burly armed men. As the riders approached, the guards strode forward; their expressions stern, their flintlocks at the ready.

'Who are you?' asked the first man, gruffly.

'Kindly tell Colonel Chivers that Mr McCloud is here to see him,' said Fraser, drawing his horse to a halt.

'The colonel's not expecting visitors,' said the other man, a stolid-looking fellow with a black beard.

'I believe he'll see me,' said Fraser, making it clear that he wasn't going to be turned away. So, after some hesitation, the gates were opened and the bearded man stepped inside. He ran up the drive towards the house, while his companion stood regarding the three riders in a surly manner, chewing on a wad of tobacco as he did so. After what seemed like hours, his companion came running back, waving an arm to indicate that the visitors should be admitted.

'In you go,' said the first man, looking somewhat disappointed.

Fraser and Callum urged their horses forward, but Mhairi made no attempt to go with them.

'If it's all the same to you,' she told Fraser, 'I'd prefer to wait here.'

He gave her an indifferent look. 'Suit yourself,' he said, and rode through the gap in the gates. Callum threw an anxious look back at Mhairi as he followed Fraser, but her face was expressionless. They rode their horses along the drive and Callum marvelled at the grandeur of the house that lay at the end of it.

He wondered how many rooms there were. Dozens, judging by the size of the place.

'Imagine living somewhere like this,' he murmured.

'Dream on,' Fraser advised him. 'Such luxury is not for the likes of you and me. A man has to be born into such wealth.' He looked at Callum. 'Why do you suppose the girl didn't want to come with us?'

Callum had a pretty good idea, but didn't want to say too much. 'I don't think she has a good opinion of Colonel Chivers,' he said, and left it at that.

'She wants to be careful,' muttered Fraser. 'The likes of her do not go around criticising the likes of the colonel. He's a powerful man in these parts.'

*Powerful, but secretive*, thought Callum.

As they neared the end of the drive, they saw Colonel Chivers awaiting them at the top of a long flight of stone steps. A liveried servant stood beside him and as Fraser and Callum dismounted, he came down the steps to take the horses' reins. The colonel followed.

'Gentlemen,' he said. 'This is an unexpected pleasure.' He waved a hand around him. 'As it's a pleasant day, I thought we might talk out here in the grounds. It's about time for my daily stroll, anyway.'

Callum couldn't help feeling a twinge of disappointment. He'd really been looking forward to seeing if the inside of the building was as opulent as its exterior. Fraser didn't seem to mind. He nodded, and he and Callum fell into step with the old man as he led them around the side of the house, through a meticulously groomed yew arch and into a huge formal garden, planted with beautiful flowers and studded with statues, tall stone or bronze figures representing half naked warriors and women wearing even less. Callum hardly knew which way to look.

'How is the hunt progressing?' asked the colonel.

'It's not,' said Fraser, bluntly. 'Clues seem to be in very short supply.'

'Oh, dear.' The colonel frowned. 'Then your presence here is puzzling. I was hoping you had some good news for me.'

'Forgive my frankness, Colonel Chivers, but I don't believe you've been entirely honest with me.'

The colonel raised his bushy eyebrows. 'Is that so, Mr McCloud?'

'Yes, sir, it is. When you first called to my home and told me about the situation here, I rather think you omitted to give me all of the details.'

'Did I indeed?' The colonel gave him a look of exaggerated innocence.

'I was led to believe, sir, that this mysterious beast you wish me to hunt down, had been preying mostly on livestock and that Mr Gilmour was the only human being who was missing.'

'Is that the impression you got?' Colonel Chivers feigned surprise. 'I can't imagine what gave you that idea.'

'Now I am told that, in fact, three other people have vanished – four, if we count Mrs Gilmour.'

'Ah, so there was no sign of a body in the croft?' The colonel looked troubled by this news. 'I had a report that there'd been some kind of incident and I sent Michael straight out to find you.' He seemed to remember something. 'She had a couple of children, did she not?'

'She did, sir. They are safe and well with a neighbour. But of Mrs Gilmour, there's not so much as a hair. And . . . something doesn't make sense about the attack. The door had been smashed to pieces and the croft was wrecked inside, but there were none of the traces I'd expect to find after an animal attack.'

'Such as?'

'Bloodstains, drag marks, tracks leading in and out . . .'

'There was the bite taken out of that table,' Callum reminded him.

'Aye.' Fraser looked at the colonel. 'The boy speaks true. Whatever this creature is, it had bitten a chunk out of a solid oak table.' Fraser held his hands a foot apart. 'A chunk this size. Now, you tell me, Colonel, do you know of any wolf capable of such a thing?'

Colonel Chivers shrugged his shoulders. 'I am no expert on wolves, Mr McCloud. That's why I hired you.' He stopped walking for a moment and studied Fraser intently. 'Please tell me you're not coming around to the local opinion. All that nonsense about a faerie hound and wood walkers.'

'No. Of course not. Except . . .'

'Except what, Mr McCloud?'

'I'm just trying to establish a pattern here. What can you tell me about the other missing people?'

The colonel started walking again and Fraser and Callum were obliged to hurry after him. 'There *is* no pattern,' said Colonel Chivers. 'They were just three crofters from the estate, with nothing at all in common . . .'

'Except they all helped to clear forest land so you could build on it,' said Callum impulsively, and was rewarded with a glare from both his companions.

'Where did you get that from?' muttered Fraser.

'I ... overheard people saying it ... at the inn.'

Fraser glanced at the colonel. 'That's not true, is it?'

The old man looked evasive. 'Well, yes, it *is*, actually, but . . . it means nothing. There were plenty of locals who helped with that task. And they were all happy to have the work, I might add.'

'But they all took money from you, didn't they?' said Callum. 'And so did Mrs Gilmour. She said—'

He broke off in alarm as Fraser gave him a powerful slap across the back of his head, almost knocking him off his feet.

'Watch how you speak to the colonel!' he snarled. 'It's not your place to be questioning him in such an impudent manner.'

Callum lifted a hand to massage the back of his head. 'Sorry,' he muttered. 'I forgot myself.'

The colonel waved a hand to dismiss his worries. 'No matter,' he said. 'And I won't pretend that what the boy says isn't true. Of course, I gave her something for her troubles. I felt sorry for her and wanted to help.' He sighed. 'Furthermore, I don't feel I've done anything wrong in this regard. The land was mine to do with as I pleased and, as it happened, it pleased me to clear some of it to build a hunting lodge. That's not a crime, is it?'

'Of course not,' said Fraser.

'But to hear some of the locals speak of it, you'd think that land belonged to somebody else . . . these mysterious 'walkers' they are so fond of mentioning. It's hard to believe, but many of the people hereabouts troop regularly into that forest to visit some old well . . .'

'The Clootie Well,' murmured Callum, and once again was aware of Fraser shooting him a suspicious look.

'. . . where they make ridiculous offerings to some ancient

forest deity in the belief that their deepest wishes will be granted.' The colonel scoffed. 'I mean, this is the eighteenth century, for goodness' sake! We've all moved on, haven't we?' He seemed to consider for a moment and then let out a sigh. 'Mr McCloud, I must admit that you are correct in your assumption. There *is* more to this story than I've previously let on.'

Fraser raised his eyebrows. 'Why would you withhold information from me?' he protested.

'Because it's . . . not for everyone to know. A delicate matter.' The colonel spread his hands. 'Very well, I'll share it with you, but only on the understanding that you keep it to yourselves.' He looked at Fraser and then at Callum. 'I want your solemn promise – both of you – that what you are about to hear goes no further. Do I have that promise?'

'Of course,' said Fraser. He glared at Callum and nudged him hard with an elbow.

'Er . . . aye,' said Callum. 'I promise, sir.'

'Come with me.' The colonel changed direction and followed a flagged path across a broad expanse of lawn to a long, low building which Callum initially supposed to be a stable. But, when they went through the open doors, they heard the sound of barking and saw that a whole troop of hunting dogs were housed behind bars. At the sight of visitors, the dogs started up a clamour, until a huge, muscular man with a shaven head appeared from around the side of a cage and lashed at the bars with a leather riding crop.

'Quiet!' he roared. 'Quieten down, you noisy mutts!' The man had what Callum thought might be an Irish accent and the effect he had on the dogs was dramatic. They instantly quietened down and sank into submissive postures; their heads bowed, their tails tucked between their legs. It was evident at a glance that the dogs were afraid of this man and of the crop he carried.

He turned away from the cage and approached the visitors, bowing politely.

'Good day to you, Colonel,' he said.

'Good day, Declan. These gentlemen have come here to help with the little matter of the, er, wolf. But after much consideration, I've decided I'd like you to tell them about Chaser.'

Declan looked taken aback. 'What . . . everything?' he murmured.

Colonel Chivers nodded. 'Everything,' he said. 'Leave nothing out.'

'Very good, sir. If you're sure.' Declan seemed to consider for a while before he spoke. Callum noticed that the man had a gold ring through one ear and that there was a tattoo on his neck, the image of a cross, from which hung a set of scales.

'It was perhaps four years ago,' he said. 'I chanced to be visiting my homeland and I knew that the colonel was after getting his hands on a good hunting dog, something that would be suitable for going after deer.'

He paused and glanced at the colonel, as though still unsure about continuing, but the old man waved a hand to give his assent.

'There was a fellow I knew out in Roscommon who bred Irish wolfhounds, so I went to see him and he told me that one of his best dogs had just had a litter of puppies. I went along and had a look at them. There was one particular pup that took my fancy, much bigger than his brothers and sisters, huge paws on him. My friend warned me to pick one of the others – he thought there was something not quite right with this feller – but I liked the look of the pup, so I paid good coin for him and brought him back to Scotland with me.'

He glanced at the colonel once more, as though checking again that he wasn't saying too much.

'Well, I named him Chaser and he grew fast. When only a year old he was the biggest dog I'd ever seen, but he had a mean streak on him. I couldn't train him no matter how hard I beat him . . .'

'You beat him?' Callum couldn't stop himself from speaking out. 'I was always taught that you train an animal with kindness!'

Declan winked at Fraser. 'Looks like we have an expert with us!' he observed, mockingly, and reached out a hand to ruffle Callum's hair. 'No, sonny, this was no lapdog . . . he was a giant. By the time he was fully grown, he was the height of your shoulder and he had jaws that could rip a deer's leg off without any effort. You don't fool around with a beast like that, you have to let him know who's master.'

'Hear, hear,' said Colonel Chivers. 'Go on, Declan.'

'Well, we took him out after deer several times, didn't we? He was a matchless hunter, but the sight of blood seemed to send him into some kind of frenzy, and you just couldn't call him off when he was like that. I said to the colonel, several times, that maybe we should cut our losses and put him down. But we both kept thinking that maybe he'd come right in the end. And then, I believe it was three months ago, we was chasing a big stag – fabulous set of antlers on him – and the stag made a break for it and ran into the forest. The other hounds stopped dead in their tracks . . . they'll never venture into that place . . .'

'Why's that?' asked Callum.

Declan shrugged his massive shoulders. 'I really cannot say. They seem to have a fear of the trees. Can't say I blame them, that place gives *me* the chills . . . but Chaser wouldn't give up.

He went in there after the stag, deep into woodland.' He scowled. 'And that's the last we seen of him. Oh, I've had a good look in there, mind, must have gone in two or three times over the months, thinking if I saw him, I'd shoot him.'

'Shoot him?' Callum realised he was risking another clout from Fraser but couldn't stop himself. 'Why would you do that?'

'Because he'd turned wild and should be put out of his misery. But without hounds to help me track him, I had no chance of finding him. That place is like a vast rabbit warren; it extends for mile after mile, and there's plenty of game in there for him to dine on. I never seen hide nor hair of him after that. And then, of course, the sheep started to be taken . . .'

Fraser let out a slow breath. 'So, you're suggesting that this . . . wolfhound . . . is our culprit?'

'Alas, it seems more than likely,' said Colonel Chivers. He nodded to Declan, dismissing him, and the man went back to whatever he'd been doing before. Colonel Chivers turned back to Fraser and Callum. 'So there you have it,' he said. 'The full story. Now, I'm sure I don't have to tell you how it would be regarded if word got out that this vicious creature had actually come from my own kennels. So, I will remind you again, gentlemen, to keep this information to yourselves. But one thing's for sure. The attacker is no supernatural beast, but an Irish wolfhound of exceptional size and strength. Furthermore, it seems to me that if you are going to have a chance of bringing him down, you will need to seek him in his lair. The Forest of Tay.'

\*\*\*

They rode slowly back to the gates. Fraser's head was bowed, and he seemed to be brooding on the conversation he'd just had.

'You could have told the colonel you wanted to be excused from this,' said Callum quietly. 'You could have given him his money back.'

Fraser gave him a look of disbelief. 'And why would I do a thing like that?' he snapped.

'Well, because he . . . he didn't give you the full story.'

'But he has now, hasn't he? And as far as I'm concerned, it's good news.'

Callum frowned. 'It is?'

'Aye. We now have proof that the creature we're hunting is real. A thing of flesh and blood. Which means it can be killed.'

'But . . . you never thought it was anything else, did you?'

Fraser gave him an odd look. 'No, of course not.' But it didn't sound very convincing. 'Anyway, now we have the truth, so . . .'

'But you saw that table, didn't you?' persisted Callum. 'The size of that bite! Do you really think—'

Fraser's expression turned abruptly to one of anger. 'You know what?' he snarled. 'I'm beginning to think that you're getting a bit too fond of questioning me. Don't forget who's the master here. Or would you like another slap around the head?'

Callum shrugged. 'No, sir,' he said. But it struck him that Fraser was just like Declan, believing that inflicting pain was the best way to make people toe the line.

Fraser lifted his head to look at the gates where Mhairi was waiting for them. 'You just apply your mind to working out how you're going to get that girl to guide us through the forest,' he suggested. 'Since she professes to be such an expert on the place, it's time we put it to the test. So, we'll head in there tonight, while we still have the hunter's moon to light our way.'

'Tonight?' Callum did not like the sound of this. He thought back to his own nocturnal visit to the place; the eerie sounds of howling coming from the depths of the forest. 'Is that wise?'

'By all accounts, that's when this creature is most active,' said Fraser. 'So that's when we should be there, ready to take him down.'

# 11

# PERSUASION

Heading back to the Shepherd's Crook, Callum took the opportunity to ride up alongside Mhairi, leaving Fraser some distance behind them.

'Why didn't you want to go into the colonel's?' Callum asked her.

'Because I didn't feel welcome there.' She looked at Callum slyly. 'Not that you two were exactly welcome either.'

Callum looked at her. 'What's that supposed to mean?'

'I saw the three of you wandering around in his garden. Funny, isn't it, he didn't invite you into his fine house?'

Callum thought about that. 'He said it was a pleasant day, so . . .'

'So, he kept the two of you standing on his lawn. You don't suppose he thought you weren't good enough to go inside? You don't think he was worried you might soil his lovely carpets and furnishings?'

'It never crossed my mind,' said Callum. 'Why do you hate him so much? He can't help being rich, can he?'

'It's not him I hate,' said Mhairi. 'It's what he stands for. People like him have this country in the palms of their hands.' She lifted one fist to gaze at it as though considering punching somebody. 'But think about it for a moment, Callum. Everything he owns is his by right of conquest. His ancestors took the land his fine house is built on. They took it from people like me and you and now we have no say in what happens to it. Is that fair?'

'I suppose not, but . . .'

'If Colonel Chivers decides it's time for us all to go hungry, then that's what happens. If he thinks he wants new tenants, well, he'll just turf us out in favour of new ones and nobody will be able to say a word about it. But he'll be all right, won't he, whatever happens? The likes of the colonel will always have everything they need, just by snapping their fingers.' She looked at Callum. 'So, what did he have to say for himself?'

Callum frowned. He knew that he'd promised not to tell anybody else about Chaser, but also knew that Fraser was counting on Mhairi to act as their guide into the forest tonight, so he lowered his voice and whispered an account of what Declan had said. As he spoke, Mhairi's eyes appeared to get bigger and bigger, as she took in the full implications of it all.

'So, you're telling me—'

'Whisht!' Callum glanced guiltily back to Fraser. 'Please don't let him know I've told you, or my life won't be worth living.'

Mhairi nodded and continued in a whisper. 'You're saying that it's the colonel himself who has brought this on us?'

'Well, yes, in a way. Him and Declan.'

'Typical! The colonel blunders and we have to pay the price for his stupidity.' Mhairi pondered for a moment and then shook her head. 'It doesn't make any kind of sense, though,' she muttered.

'What doesn't?'

'Why would this Chaser only hunt down people who have taken money from the colonel? I mean, if it's just an ordinary hound, how would it know about such things? It *is* only a dog, right?'

'A very big one, but . . . yes.' Now it was Callum's turn to ponder. 'Maybe it's a coincidence,' he suggested. 'That the three missing people . . .'

'Four,' Mhairi reminded him.

'Aye, four, then. But a coincidence that they are all people who accepted the colonel's money. He said there were lots of others who did.'

Mhairi looked at him. 'He would say that, wouldn't he?'

'But you told me pretty much the same thing yourself!'

She shrugged. 'I suppose I did. But you believe this story, do you? About the wolfhound?'

'I don't know what to believe, Mhairi. All I know . . .' He risked a quick look back at Fraser, who still seemed to be lost in his own thoughts. '. . . is that he wants to go into the forest tonight to try and shoot the creature.'

'Oh well, good luck with that,' said Mhairi scornfully.

'No, listen! Here's the thing. He's hoping you'll act as our guide.'

'Is he really?'

'You said you would before.'

She snorted. 'As I remember it, Andrew offered my services. I don't seem to recall him asking me.'

'But you didn't say no, did you? All I can tell you is it makes me nervous, the thought of going into the forest after that hound. In the dark. I already had a terrible dream about it.'

'A dream?' She looked interested now. 'Tell me.'

'It was just a nightmare.'

'Ah, no, dreams can tell us more about life than you'd imagine. Go on, tell me what happened.'

'Well, I dreamt that Fraser and me went into the Forest of Tay, after the wolf – the hound – whatever it is. We were walking through the forest at night, and I was terrified. And then we heard this awful music playing.'

'Music? What kind of music?'

'It was just a slow air.' Callum thought for a moment. 'Now I think of it, I believe it was the same tune that the old woman was singing.'

She gave him a despairing look. 'What old woman?' she muttered.

'Oh, just a washerwoman we saw on our way to the Gilmour's croft. She was washing clothes in the river and singing this old song about "poor Johnnie" or some such nonsense. She . . .' His voice trailed away. Now Mhairi was looking at him with an expression of pure dread on her face.

'You met the washer at the ford?' she whispered.

He gazed back at her. 'Aye. Is that . . . a problem? She was just some old lady cleaning . . . well, now I think of it, she was cleaning blood out of some clothes.'

Mhairi closed her eyes for a moment. She swallowed. 'And did you happen to see what clothes they were?'

'It was . . . I think it was a man's shirt. A white one. Mhairi, why are you looking at me like that?'

'And her face?'

'Hmm?'

'Did you see her face?'

Callum shook his head. 'She had most of it covered with a scarf.' He swallowed. 'I saw her hands though. They were . . .' He saw that he didn't need to mention that the woman's fingers were webbed. The look of revulsion on Mhairi's pale face said it all. 'Who was she?' he murmured.

'The washer at the ford. Have you never heard of her? She's infamous! She cleans the clothes of people who are close to death. She keeps her face covered because she only has the one nostril.'

He thought perhaps that Mhairi was playing a joke on him and even attempted a half-hearted laugh, but it died in his throat when Mhairi's expression stayed exactly the same. 'You're being serious, aren't you? he said.

She nodded. 'Deadly serious.'

He thought frantically for a moment. 'I'm pretty sure it wasn't one of *my* shirts,' he whispered. He glanced back at Fraser. 'I think *he* has a white one, though. He keeps it for . . .' He remembered something. 'Oh, no,' he said.

'What?'

'Fraser said that shirt was missing. The night we arrived. He asked me if I knew where it was.' He stared at her. 'You don't think . . .?'

'I don't know for sure,' she assured him. 'But if I were you, I'd try to persuade Fraser to give that money back before it's too late.'

Now Callum did laugh. 'You have to be joking! There's no way in the world he'd ever do that! You may as well tell the rain to stop falling.'

'What are you two laughing about?' asked Fraser, urging his horse suddenly forward to join them. He pulled up on the far side of Mhairi.

She studied Fraser coolly for a moment before she spoke.

'Callum was asking me to guide you into the woods tonight,' she said. 'That gave me reason to laugh.'

Fraser nodded. 'And will you?' He noted her look of reluctance and added, "You'd be doing the local community a great service.'

'Would I really?'

'Of course you would. All those sheep slain, all those people missing. You'd like to see an end to that, wouldn't you?'

'I would, but I'm not sure wandering around the forest in the middle of the night is the right way to go about it.'

Fraser looked irritated. 'The colonel shared some information with us just now. I can't give you the full details, but it confirms that we're looking for a creature of flesh and blood. Not the strange beastie you and your friends keep talking so fondly about. So, all I'm asking is for you to lead us to it and I'll do the rest.'

'Oh, you will, will you? And we'll all be so grateful to you, won't we. Fraser McCloud, come to save us all from hell and damnation.'

Fraser gave her a look of disbelief. 'Somebody should have a word with you about how you address your elders,' he snarled.

'Oh, don't worry. Many people already have.'

Fraser's eyes narrowed suspiciously. 'Ah, I get it. You're holding out for payment, are you? Well, it's not out of the question. How much do you want?'

Mhairi glared at him. 'I didn't mention money,' she protested.

'You didn't have to. So, I'll ask again. How much?'

She shook her head in despair. 'I don't want a penny from you,' she assured him. 'I'm not that stupid. I know that it comes from the colonel's purse. But I will guide you, if only to look out for that one.' She nodded towards Callum. 'I'm not sure why, but I've taken a bit of a shine to him.'

Fraser smiled mirthlessly. 'But you're not so keen on me?' he murmured. 'Is that what you're trying to say?'

'I'm not trying to say anything, Mr McCloud,' she told him. 'And if I really didn't like you, make no mistake, you'd know all about it.'

With that, she dug her heels into Blizzard's flanks and galloped onwards. Callum gazed after her. Beyond her, across the wide expanse of moorland, he could see the distant outline of the Shepherd's Crook.

'That one has too high an opinion of herself,' observed Fraser. 'She'd want to be careful, speaking to her superiors like that. But we need her, so for now, I'm going to resist taking my riding crop to her.' He shot Callum a barbed look. 'What were the two of you discussing so avidly?'

Callum shrugged. 'She was telling me about the old woman.'

'Which old woman?'

'The one we saw at the river just before we got to the Gilmour's croft.'

Fraser narrowed his eyes suspiciously. 'What about her?' he growled.

'She was . . .' For some reason, Callum couldn't bring himself to repeat what Mhairi had told him. He could already picture Fraser's contemptuous expression. 'She was Mhairi's cousin. She lives near there.'

Fraser grunted. 'Imagine being related to that minx,' he muttered. 'I wouldn't wish that on anyone.' He reached out and stroked his horse's mane. 'For a moment there, I thought you were about to feed me some kind of superstitious nonsense.'

Callum looked away. 'Not me,' he murmured.

'Good. This new information we've been given makes me feel a whole lot happier about this business,' continued Fraser.

'Does it really?' muttered Callum.

'Aye, it does. Here's what's going to happen. We'll head back to the inn and we'll avail ourselves of some hot food and a tankard of ale apiece. We'll get a couple of hours' shut-eye and then we'll head out into those woods.'

Callum frowned. 'But, by all accounts, they are *massive*,' he said. 'How are we going to find one hound in the middle of all that? It'll be like looking for a needle in a haystack.'

Fraser shook his head. 'No, it won't. I've been thinking it through. You're right, it's pointless to go wandering around looking for the creature, hoping to chance upon it. What are the odds? No, Hamish Gilmour had the right idea, it just didn't go quite to plan.'

Callum frowned. 'I don't understand,' he said.

'It's very simple, lad. We just need to offer our predator the right kind of bait. And then, he'll come to us.'

# 12

# CURSED

When Callum and Fraser rode into the cobbled courtyard of the Shepherd's Crook, there was no sign of Mhairi, who must have arrived well ahead of them. They dismounted, and Fraser handed Callum the reins of the two horses.

'I'm heading inside for a drink,' he announced. 'Get these ladies to that good-for-nothing ostler and make sure you tell him we'll be needing them, saddled and ready, later on tonight.' And with that he strode across to the front entrance of the inn and went in through the door.

Callum performed a comical bow. 'Very good, sir,' he said, adopting the voice of a servant. 'No, no, don't mention it, it's my pleasure!' But he made sure to keep his voice low enough so it wouldn't be heard inside the inn.

He sighed, then turned and led the horses towards the open doors of the stable. As he approached, he heard voices coming from inside and instantly recognised the tobacco-coursened croak of old Tam.

'. . . and I'm telling you, ya wee whelp, I know you did something to me! I slept like a dead man the whole night and I had dreams such as I've never had! And when have you ever bothered yourself to bring me out a mug of wine before, eh? What did you put in that drink?'

Callum hurried into the stable and saw that Tam had Mhairi pinned up against a barrel, one hand clutching the fabric of her dress just below her throat. She was gazing steadily back at him, her calm expression mocking him.

'You're just getting old, Tam,' she assured him. 'Old people sleep more than young ones. Why is that such a hard notion to understand?'

'Why, you damned shargie. Somebody ought to teach you better manners.' Tam lifted his left hand with the intention of striking her, but Callum stilled him with a shout.

'What are you doing?' he cried. 'Take your hands off her!'

Tam twisted around to look at Callum, and his face collapsed into something that was probably intended as a grin but which came across as a bizarre grimace.

'I might have known you'd turn up,' he sneered. 'The faithful follower.' Callum noticed the old man's speech was slurred and even at this distance he could smell the heady aroma of ale coming off him. 'If the girl told you black was white, you'd believe her. The shargie has you enchanted, boy, can't you see that?'

Callum let go of the horses' reins and strode nearer. 'Stop calling her that,' he said. 'She can't help being a foundling.'

'A foundling? Is that what you think it means?' Tam laughed. 'Not so much a foundling as a *changeling*, eh, Mhairi?' He turned back to look at her. 'The spawn of the wood walkers handed over to us mortals to care for. It's the age-old story, isn't it?'

'Be quiet,' she advised him. 'You're stinking drunk, and you need to go and sleep it off.'

'Like you made me sleep last night?' he said. 'Slipping some magical potion into my drink. I ought to give you a good beating for doing that to me.' Again, he raised his left hand and Callum stepped quickly forward to grab his shoulders – then reeled away with a yelp as Tam spun around and punched him on the jaw. Callum went down on his back, falling perilously close to the restless hooves of the horses. He had to roll frantically aside to avoid being trampled. Tam advanced on him, his fists raised, his expression triumphant. 'Come on, you wee pup. I'll show you how a man handles these things,' he bellowed.

'You, sir!' snapped Mhairi, and something in her voice caused Tam to spin back around. The girl was staring at him with those unsettling eyes and her face was now a mask of hatred. 'You have gone too far,' she hissed. 'Now you have made me angry. And when I'm angry, I talk to my friends in the forest, and I tell them to avenge me.'

Quite suddenly, all the fight went out of old Tam, like water flooding out of a broken barrel. He lowered his fists and stared at Mhairi, slack-jawed. 'You . . . wouldn't do that,' he protested.

'Oh, wouldn't I? Of course I would! I'd ask them to spin me a curse, a really powerful one, a curse that I could place on the head of anyone who offended me. I would . . . wait!' She cocked her head to one side and affected an unfocussed look. 'They are speaking to me now,' she whispered.

Tam looked in the direction in which she was staring. 'What . . . what are they saying?' he whispered.

Mhairi ignored him. She was nodding, as though listening to voices. 'Aye,' she crooned. 'That's the one. The old ostler. The one they call Tam. He has disrespected me.'

Tam shook his head. 'No,' he murmured. 'Don't say any more, please.'

'He has accused me of things I haven't done . . . and worst of all, he knows of our secret.'

Even though the sting of Tam's blow still bothered him, Callum lay in the straw, trying not to laugh. Mhairi was playing the old man like a concertina. Now, her eyes widened, as though she'd just received instructions. 'Do you really think so?' she whispered. 'But he is so old . . .' She nodded. 'Oh, very well then. If you insist.' She transferred her attention to the ostler and pointed an accusing finger at him. 'Old Tam,' she droned, in a toneless voice. 'I curse thee. You shall have but one day more on this earth and then you must prepare to meet your maker.'

'No!' Tam shook his head. 'No, that's not fair! Tell them I'm sorry,' he whispered. 'Please! Tell them I didn't mean any offence!'

Mhairi shook her head and affected a mournful look. 'Too late,' she moaned. 'They are gone now. Too late for you, I'm afraid. What a pity. Poor Tam. Who will mourn you when you're gone?'

Tam let out a kind of strangled cry. He spun on his heels and blundered away, past the restless horses and out through the stable door. Callum stared after him, listening to the sound of the old man's feet thudding across the cobbles as he ran. Then he turned in surprise at the sound of laughter. Mhairi was chuckling, pointing towards the stable doors. 'Did you see him move?' she cried. 'I bet that old buzzard hasn't run that fast in years!'

'Mhairi,' he murmured. 'I don't think you should have . . .'

'Oh, come on, he asked for that! Accusing me of putting

a potion in his drink. I mean, the cheek of the man.' She strode forward and reached down to help Callum to his feet. He gave her a questioning look.

'Are you honestly saying that you didn't do that?' he asked her.

She gave him an evasive look. 'That's not the point, is it?' she said. 'The thing is that he believed me capable of doing so.'

Callum stared at her. 'But . . . I don't . . .'

'Here, let's have a look at you.' She put a thumb and forefinger to his chin and guided him closer, then peered at his face. 'You're going to have quite a bruise,' she told him. 'I've some ointment that will help with that.'

He stared back at her, strangely thrilled to be so close to her. He found himself unaccountably breathless. 'I just . . . don't think it was a good idea to . . . to curse him like that.'

'Why?' She grinned. 'Are you afraid it might work?'

'No, of course not, but . . .'

'I suppose I should thank you,' she murmured.

'For what?'

'For coming to my rescue. Like a hero. A knight in shining armour.'

'Some hero,' he protested. 'The old man knocked me flat on my back.'

'He caught you by surprise, that's all. Besides, heroism should always be rewarded, don't you think?'

There was a moment of silence so deep, Callum thought that he could hear the beating of his own heart in his chest. Then she leant that little bit closer and brushed her lips against his. A series of shocks jittered through him from head to foot. She held him there for a moment and then moved away a little.

She smiled at the shocked expression on his face. 'Now then,' she said. She lifted a hand to touch the red spot on his cheek. 'How does it feel?'

'Better,' he said.

The spell was broken and they moved apart, both of them suddenly self-conscious.

'Well,' said Mhairi. 'I'd better get on. There's the supper to attend to.'

'Yes. And I'll get these horses stabled,' said Callum, aware that his voice was much louder than it needed to be. 'Now that you've scared the ostler away,' he added. 'You've made extra work for me.'

She chuckled and went to move past him, but he placed a hand on her shoulder and held her there for a moment. 'Before you go,' he murmured. 'Perhaps . . . one more kiss?'

She studied him for a moment, then smiled. 'Why not?' she said, and moved back into his arms.

# 13

# BAIT

The three of them rode slowly across the moor. Above them, the great red orb of the hunter's moon gazed impassively down on them. Callum clung grimly on to the length of rope in his left hand and tried to ignore the constant bleating of the kid goat that he was leading along behind him.

'Did it really have to be so young?' he asked Fraser, for perhaps the fourth time.

'Whisht, boy, I've already told you. The wee goat's perfect – he's going to be calling for his mother all night long. And that's exactly what we need to lure the hound to us. Don't worry, I'll shoot the beast dead long before it ever gets close enough to take a bite.'

Callum frowned. 'What if you miss?' he asked.

'I never miss,' said Fraser. 'Wasn't I my regiment's finest sharpshooter? Didn't they present me with a medal for it?'

Callum didn't have an answer for that. He couldn't help wondering why he'd never seen such a medal. It wasn't as if Fraser was shy about his past. He'd once proudly shown Callum a moth-eaten old uniform stored in a wooden trunk, together with a rusting sword, but that was the only evidence that Callum had ever seen of his master's supposedly glorious military career.

If he'd had any medals, then he must have sold them when times were hard.

Callum transferred his attention to Mhairi, who rode slightly ahead of them, wrapped in a voluminous hooded cloak. She hadn't said much since they'd set off. Back at the inn, Andrew had taken the news that his 'daughter' was to lead the two hunters into the Forest of Tay without any complaint, but he had been quick to enquire how much she was to be paid for her services.

'I don't want to be paid,' she'd insisted, and Andrew had looked at her as though she was mad.

'I'm sure Mr McCloud doesn't expect you to risk your life for nothing,' he said. He looked at Callum. 'And I'm sure *you* get paid for your services, don't you?' There was an uncomfortable silence before Mhairi said, 'It's already settled, Andrew. I'm not taking a penny and there's an end to it. Now, if you'll excuse me, I've the supper to attend to.'

She'd seemed resolved to the task back then, but now, riding slowly towards the forest, Callum wondered if Mhairi was having second thoughts about the whole enterprise. What he could see of her face in the shadow of the hood looked decidedly moody. Callum thought about what had happened in the stable earlier and realised that he was beginning to care very much about this girl's feelings.

The three riders crested the ridge and gazed down once again at the jagged stretch of cleared land that lay between them and the forest. Mhairi seemed to come out of her reverie and looked at Fraser. 'So,' she said, 'Where exactly do you want me to take you?' She pointed to the great swathe of vegetation ahead of them. 'There are miles and miles to choose from and I know every inch of it.'

Callum thought that Fraser wouldn't have a clue about that, but he'd evidently been thinking it over as he'd eaten his supper.

'We need somewhere with a supply of fresh drinking water,' he said. 'Somewhere with a bit of height where I can look down upon the tethered goat and have a clear shot at whatever might approach. Do you know of a spot that fits that description?'

She thought for a moment and then nodded. 'I think I do. Follow me.' She urged Blizzard over the crest of the hill and down the other side. Fraser and Callum followed.

'Drinking water?' asked Callum. 'We have that in our canteens.'

Fraser shook his head. 'It's not for *us*, you dummy. It's for the hound.'

'For the hound? You're going to offer it a drink?'

Fraser looked annoyed. 'Do you do it on purpose?' he asked. He shook his head. 'When an animal has devoured red meat, it soon needs to slake its thirst. It will often drag a carcass closer to water before it starts to eat. Everyone knows that.'

Callum looked at him blankly. 'It's news to me,' he admitted.

'It's just common sense. If we place our bait close to somewhere the hound can drink straight afterwards, it'll be doubly enticing.'

Callum gazed down at the miserable, bleating kid who was looking up at him as if imploring mercy. He didn't care for that word. *Bait*. 'But you *will* kill the hound before he can get to the goat?'

Fraser rolled his eyes. 'How many more times? Don't worry, I have every intention of bringing your wee friend back in one piece. Otherwise, I'll lose the deposit the farmer insisted on me paying before I borrowed him for the night. Damned thief!'

They rode slowly past the stone spiral and Callum found himself staring at it, trying to imagine what the mysterious 'walkers' must look like as they moved around it, chanting their faerie songs. Were they ordinary-looking people, or wee hobgoblins with pointed ears and hook noses? Did they even exist or were they just the product of people's imaginations? Mhairi seemed to believe in them . . . at least, he *thought* she did. She had never denied their existence, but neither had she come right out and said that they were real. The troubling thing about Mhairi was that the more he found out about her, the less he seemed to know.

She veered her horse to the left and entered the edge of the forest where a narrow track led onwards into the gloom. Callum took a last anxious look around, before following her into the undergrowth. Behind him, the goat gave a last, despairing bleat as darkness engulfed them.

***

'Is this what you were thinking of?' asked Mhairi, reining Blizzard to a halt.

They had ridden for what seemed like hours, each twisting track turning into another, until Callum had no idea of where he was any more. But the clearing that they had just come into seemed to fit Fraser's description perfectly and it was a relief to be once again bathed in moonlight. A large outcrop of grey stone stuck up from the ground, overlooking a place where a restless stream slowed to enter a shallow pool of water. Once it had reached its level, the stream cascaded onwards, tumbling down a steep slope and off into the trees. Fraser nodded. 'This is perfect,' he said. 'A good vantage point, with fresh water and plenty of moonlight. I couldn't ask for a better spot. How can it be that you know this vast place so well?'

She shrugged. 'I love it here,' she said. 'And I've made it my business to explore every inch of it.'

Fraser pointed to the top of the stone mound. 'We'll take up a position on top of that,' he said. 'There, where there's a bit of rock to hide us from view. And we'll tether the goat down here, right beside the pool.'

'What about the horses?' asked Mhairi.

'Put them in that gully,' suggested Fraser, indicating a deep cleft in the base of the rock. 'And heap branches and the like at the entrance so they're hidden from sight.' He seemed pleased with his plan. 'Callum, you stake out the goat. Mhairi, you take care of the horses.'

'And what will you be doing?' asked Mhairi, giving him a critical look.

'I'll be up there, preparing the guns,' said Fraser. He climbed down from the saddle and withdrew his flintlock from its holder. He studied the rocks for a moment and then started walking to what looked like the easiest place to climb. 'Come and join me when you're both finished,' he told his companions. He glanced back at Callum. 'Make sure you tie that goat so it can't get away,' he warned. 'Otherwise, you'll be taking his place.'

Callum hoped that this was intended as a joke, but as ever with Fraser, he couldn't really be sure. He climbed down from Molly, collected the wooden peg and mallet he'd brought with him from the inn and handed the reins over to Mhairi, who led all three horses away.

'I love the way we get to do all the donkey work,' she muttered under her breath, and she and Callum shared a knowing smile. Callum walked the little goat across to the pool and stooped down to pat its head. He looked up at Fraser, who was already climbing.

'Here?' he suggested, pointing at the ground.

'Wait till I'm up at the top,' suggested Fraser. 'I'll have a better idea when I'm in position.'

The goat gazed up at Callum and gave another plaintive cry, as if asking to be spared his part in the plan. For the first time, Callum noticed how unsettling the little creature's eyes were – pure orange orbs with a thick black line where the pupil ought to be. In the full moonlight, they were almost demonic. Callum looked away – not wanting to dwell on the thought.

'Now then . . .' Fraser's head appeared over the top of a stone outcrop. He swung the gun into view and pointed it towards the goat. Callum flinched.

'Be careful with that thing,' he said.

'Relax. It's not even loaded yet. Move the goat a wee bit to the right . . . a bit more . . . that's perfect. Tether him there.'

Callum stabbed the end of the peg into the ground and, lifting the mallet, he started to hammer the thing into position. The goat watched, bewildered.

'Come on, lad, put some effort into it!' he heard Fraser shout, and for a moment Callum imagined that he was pounding his employer's head with the mallet. That seemed to help. The stake sank deep into the ground and in a matter of moments the goat was fixed firmly in position.

'A penny for your thoughts,' said a voice right next to Callum and he glanced guiltily up to see Mhairi smiling down at him. 'If you're finished there, you can come and help me with these horses,' she suggested, and he got back to his feet.

She glanced up to the rock where Fraser was busying himself loading his rifle and she let out a sigh. 'Something tells me this is going to be a long night,' she murmured.

*** 

Callum opened his eyes, took a moment to register where he was, then pulled the blanket tighter around him. He glanced to his left, where Mhairi had settled herself. She appeared to be fast asleep, her own blanket pulled up to her chin, her head resting against a smooth slab of stone. To his right, Fraser sat in position, his back ramrod straight as he gazed down the long barrel of his rifle at the ground below. The tethered goat was still letting out a pathetic cry every few moments.

Callum wondered what time it was. He'd managed to snatch a few moments of light sleep but was so cold, he couldn't seem to settle, and besides, now there was a more pressing need, one that was made worse by the sound of the stream tumbling restlessly over rocks. He tried to put the thought out of his mind, but couldn't. Finally, he reached out a hand and tapped Fraser on the shoulder. Fraser looked at him, irritably.

'What's wrong?' he hissed.

'I need to make water!'

'No, you don't.'

'Believe me, I do!'

Fraser scowled. 'Just hold it in,' he suggested.

'I can't.'

'Well then, pee off the side of the rock.'

Callum glanced towards Mhairi and shook his head. 'I'm not doing that!' he protested. 'What if she wakes up and sees me. I need to climb down.'

Fraser looked heavenwards and suppressed a groan. 'Go on, then. But don't be long about it.'

Callum nodded. He flung off the blanket and managed to get upright on legs that ached with the cold. He was aware of his breath clouding in front of his face. 'Maybe the hound isn't around tonight,' he muttered.

'Whisht! Go and relieve yourself and come straight back.'

Callum started to clamber down from his perch, placing his feet carefully on the slippery rock, using his hands to let himself down. He made it safely to ground level and saw that the goat had turned its head to look at him.

'I have my own problems,' Callum assured him and looked around for a place to conceal himself. He spotted an opening in some trees a few yards to his left and started towards them.

'Where are you going?' he heard Fraser whisper. 'Just do it where you stand, boy!'

Callum shook his head, still worried that Mhairi might wake up and look down over the edge of the rock. He at least wanted to be concealed from view. He ignored Fraser and hurried towards the trees, then slipped gratefully into the shadows. He found a suitable spot and began to fumble with his belt but froze when he became aware of something moving in the undergrowth a short distance ahead of him. He snatched in a breath and peered intently into the darkness. At first, he saw nothing and told himself it had just been his imagination working overtime. He reached again to his belt and again he froze, because now he thought he could see something moving in the midst of the bushes, a lighter patch of shadow crossing a darker one. He shook his head. No, it was his mind playing tricks. He just needed to pass water and get back to ...

A chill rippled through him as he registered that something heavy was pushing through leaves directly ahead of him. He nearly strained his eyes staring into the shadows and then, quite suddenly, everything came into focus. A ray of moonlight glinted on two round orbs that were staring intently at him from cover. He recognised them as eyes, only seconds before he heard a sound that nearly stopped his heart – a deep-throated, rumbling growl. The hairs on the back of his neck stood on end and he opened his mouth to let out a scream, but it died in his throat. Whatever was hidden in those bushes was lurching forwards, pushing green fronds aside. Callum had a brief impression of shaggy grey fur and bared teeth, glinting in the moonlight.

Survival instincts kicked in and he spun on his heels and started to run, but he caught his foot on a gnarled root and almost fell headlong. Somehow, he managed to correct himself, to stay upright, horribly aware now that the creature was powering itself along in pursuit.

Ahead of him, he could see the goat looking towards him, its weird eyes bulging as it saw Callum and then refocused on the thing that was following on his heels. The goat's plaintive bleat turned abruptly to a shriek of terror. Callum ran for his life and heard Fraser yelling, 'Get out the way, you fool, you're blocking my shot!' Callum knew in that instant that he had but one chance and he took it, flinging himself headlong to one side. Even before he hit the ground, he heard the roar of the flintlock, glimpsed a flash of yellow light from somewhere up above him and heard a weird yelp from behind – but then he was hit by a powerful impact as something big went crashing into him, a massive paw raking the back of his head, grazing his flesh, making him cry out in panic. Whatever it was, turned in the air, hit the ground hard and rolled over twice, before lying still.

There was a moment of deep silence. Callum dared to lift his head and look at the creature that lay stretched out on its side a few feet in front of him. He saw that it was indeed a thing of flesh and blood; a huge shaggy hound, with dark grey fur, long limbs and open jaws from which a pink tongue lolled. Blood spilt from a fresh wound in its chest and Callum also noticed another wound, half-healed, in its side – the flesh black and infected. Callum got slowly to his feet and stood there, unable to take his eyes off the creature. It was massive – surely the biggest dog he had ever seen. He was about to take another step when he heard a sound coming from the wolfhound; a low, tortured panting. To his absolute horror, he realised that the creature wasn't dead. The eyes were still animated and now the beast was moving once more, rolling slowly around to get back on to its paws. Its gaze focused and fixed intently on Callum.

'You've not killed it,' croaked Callum helplessly. 'Shoot it again.'

'It's out of pistol range,' said Fraser, his voice disconcertingly calm under the circumstances. 'I'm reloading the rifle.'

Callum considered running but knew the hound would be on him before he could take three steps – and besides, he was rooted in place by terror. He stood where he was, like a statue, his heart pounding within him, and told himself to be ready for the end. Then he heard a clear voice speaking from just a short distance away.

'Hey there, Mr Wolfhound!' The dog snapped its head around to look and Callum followed its gaze. Mhairi had come down from the rock and was walking slowly towards the injured dog, one hand extended towards it as if bidding it come to her. 'Here, boy,' she murmured. 'Good boy.'

'Mhairi, don't,' whispered Callum, and the dog switched its gaze back to its original target, lifting itself up on to its haunches.

'No, you don't want him,' said Mhairi urgently. 'Look at *me*! I'd taste far better. Come on now, there's a good boy. What are you waiting for?'

The hound's dark eyes seemed to soften into an expression of bafflement. For a moment, Callum actually thought the girl's calm voice had pacified it. But then its lips curled back, revealing rows of jagged ivory and it lunged towards her.

'Mhairi! NO!'

Callum's words were drowned by the sound of a second shot and the wolfhound stopped in its tracks and fell down like a puppet with severed strings. The long legs crumpled uselessly beneath it, and this time the open eyes were vacant. Callum looked towards the rock and saw Fraser getting to his feet, a triumphant grin on his face and, for the first time ever, Callum was delighted to see it. He turned his gaze to Mhairi. She was looking down at the dead hound, one hand still extended towards it. The look on her face was one of disappointment, Callum thought, as though she'd actually wanted the beast to take her.

'Why did you do that?' he whispered.

'You looked like you needed help,' she told him. 'What were you doing down here anyway?'

'Oh, I just needed to . . .' He glanced down, and felt his face reddening. In all the excitement, nature had taken its course and the front of his trousers were soaking wet. He turned instinctively away from her, not wanting her to see. But she was kneeling beside the dead hound now, one hand extended to stroke one of its ears. 'The poor thing,' she said. She indicated the festering wound in its side. 'Someone else must already have put a shot into it. Hamish Gilmour, I suppose. It must have been in agony.'

Footsteps thudded across the ground and Fraser ran over to them, a loaded pistol in his hand. 'You shouldn't get so close,' he warned Mhairi. 'It could be shamming. Wild beasts do that sometimes. You're supposed to throw rocks at it before you approach.'

'There's no need for that,' she assured him. 'It's dead.'

Fraser covered the last few yards and placed a boot victoriously on the hound's head. He adopted a heroic posture. 'Did you see that second shot?' he cried. 'Killed him instantly!' He looked down gloatingly on his kill. 'Now they'll have to eat their words!' he cried. 'Callum, fetch some more rope. We'll get this brute back to the town square and show everyone what's really been preying upon them. The *Cù Sìth* . . . hah!'

Mhairi reached suddenly forward and pushed Fraser's foot off the beast's head, almost making him fall over. 'Whatever he's done, he deserves to be treated with some respect!' she snarled. She jumped to her feet and stalked angrily back towards the stone outcrop, her hands on her hips. Fraser looked after her, baffled.

'What's wrong with her?' he complained. 'You'd think she'd be grateful. She was very nearly done for.' He turned towards Callum, who was still facing away from him. 'Have you gone deaf or something? I told you to fetch a rope and . . .'

Callum turned slowly around and Fraser saw what had happened to him. His mouth stretched into a mocking grin. 'Oh, dear,' he said. 'Looks like somebody didn't get to the trees in time.'

'It's not funny!' snapped Callum, wiping the grin off Fraser's face in an instant. 'Mhairi's right about you. You have no respect for anyone.' He marched the short distance to the pool, waded into it and sat down in the freezing cold water, crossing his arms in front of him. Fraser stood there, looking from Mhairi to Callum and back again, a look of complete bewilderment on his face.

'Well,' he said. 'That's marvellous, isn't it? I wasn't expecting much, but a simple "congratulations" wouldn't go amiss!'

Neither Callum nor Mhairi answered him. There was just one grateful bleat from the goat to mark his victory.

# 14
# PROOF

By the time they'd ridden the dead hound's carcass all the way back through the woods and across the moor, the sun had risen and was blazing down from a clear blue sky. Fraser and Callum had first wrapped the hound's massive carcass in blankets, then they'd lifted it across Molly's withers and tied it into position. Callum had been obliged to ride back with the dead creature right behind him, a deeply unsettling feeling. He knew it was dead but somehow couldn't rid himself of the idea that it might suddenly be reanimated. Mhairi had been furious that they weren't leaving it in the forest.

'Why do we have to parade it around the village?' she complained. 'Isn't it enough that you've killed it?'

'Of course it's not enough,' Fraser told her. 'The people will need proof, won't they? It'd be an easy matter for me to ride back and tell them what I've done. But they won't believe it until they've seen it with their own eyes.'

It was market day, so when they rode into the village square, there were already several people moving around a cluster of stalls. Fraser went straight over to the old gibbet, where he unhitched the hound's carcass, unwrapped it and tied a loop of rope around its hind legs. Then he hoisted it into the air for everyone to see. It hung there, swinging in the breeze, looking even bigger in this setting – its open jaws dripping blood on to the cobbles.

The effect was dramatic. Within moments, Fraser had a small crowd of people standing around him speculating loudly about the dead beast and asking him questions about it. It wasn't long before word of mouth began to spread around the village and others came to look on in wonder. The crowd swelled in size and people converged eagerly on Fraser, wanting to shake his hand, slap him on the back, even offer to buy him a drink at the inn. He stood proudly in front of the gibbet, arms crossed, happily recounting to anyone who was interested just how he'd managed to conquer the savage beast.

Callum and Mhairi stood off at a distance, watching it all unfold.

'Look at him,' said Mhairi sullenly. 'The big hero. He's loving this.'

Callum frowned. He wasn't sure why she was being so surly. After all, Fraser's final shot had almost certainly saved her life. 'He's only done what was asked of him,' he reasoned. 'He's killed the creature that's been causing all the havoc. That's a good thing, isn't it?'

She shrugged. 'I'm not sure. It doesn't make any sense to me.'

'Oh, you mean because it attacked us, and we're not in the colonel's pay?' Callum shrugged. 'Well, maybe you were wrong about that stuff. Maybe it's all just coincidence.'

'I don't believe in coincidence,' she snarled. 'And I don't think that poor dumb animal is what Fraser has been looking for.'

'But it must be! It's hanging there, as large as life, isn't it? And it came after us. What other answer could there be?'

She wasn't really paying attention to him. 'Oh, hello,' she said. 'I might have known *he'd* show up.'

Andrew was striding into the square, carrying a large straw basket. He looked quickly around, then pushed his way through the crowd and handed Fraser a large stone flagon. Fraser gleefully uncorked it and took a hearty swig from its contents, accompanied by much cheering from the onlookers. Andrew chatted animatedly to Fraser for a few moments, then spotted Mhairi and Callum and made his way over to them.

'What are you two doing skulking over here?' he asked them. 'You should be with Mr McCloud, soaking up some of the glory.'

Mhairi made a face. 'Is that what you think it is?' she asked him. 'Glorious? A beautiful animal, shot dead.'

'A very destructive animal,' Andrew reminded her. He reached into the basket and pulled back a cloth, revealing several pies. 'Here,' he said. 'I brought some breakfast. Mr McCloud was too preoccupied to eat, but I'd say you two must have worked up an appetite. Dig in!' Callum happily accepted a pie and took a hearty bite out of it, but Mhairi shook her head.

'I'm not hungry,' she told him.

Andrew gave Callum a weary look. 'This one has always had the appetite of a sparrow,' he said. 'I keep telling her, how do you expect to find a husband if you don't put some flesh on your bones?'

Mhairi looked insulted. 'And I keep telling you, Andrew, that I don't *want* a husband.'

He ignored the comment, half-turned and waved a hand towards Chaser. 'Look at the size of that brute,' he said. 'What manner of a dog is that?'

'Irish wolfhound,' said Callum, through a mouthful of food,

and then remembered that Colonel Chivers had cautioned him not to say too much about it. 'I, er ... think,' he added.

Andrew frowned. 'Where an earth could it have come from? Such things don't run wild.'

'Can't you guess where it came from?' Mhairi asked him. 'Your precious Colonel Chivers had it as a hunting dog, didn't he? But it ran away from him and took to living in the forest. I can't say I blame it.'

Callum gave her a sharp look, trying to warn her not to say any more but it was too late for that.

Andrew seemed disturbed by the news. 'Where did you get that information from?' he asked her.

'The colonel himself told Callum,' she assured him.

Andrew looked at Callum, his eyebrows raised, and Callum had no option but to nod in agreement.

'Well, it's probably best if you don't tell anyone else about it,' said Andrew. 'He won't want it to be common knowledge.'

'I bet he won't,' said Mhairi. 'But, see, Andrew, this is what I don't understand. Why is everybody so careful not to upset the colonel? What about his tenants? What about *us*? Don't we count for anything?'

'Of course we do, Mhairi, but ... the colonel is a powerful man. We all depend on him for survival. We wouldn't want to get on the wrong side of him, would we?'

Mhairi gave a snort of disgust. 'Heaven forbid,' she said. 'Can't you see you're just putting yourself in danger, following that man's bidding?'

Andrew looked bewildered. 'How can I be in danger?' he asked. He pointed to the wolfhound's dangling body. 'Mr McCloud has put an end to such worries. You should be grateful to him!"

Mhairi scowled. 'I'm heading back to the inn,' she said. 'I'm going to try and get some sleep before I set about my duties for the day.' She gave Callum a look. 'You may as well stay here and bask in the reflected glory,' she added. And before he could offer a reply, she stalked away in the direction of the Shepherd's Crook, leading Blizzard behind her.

Andrew shook his head. 'Always been headstrong, that one,' he murmured. 'She gets a bee in her bonnet, and nothing will shift it.' He studied Callum, who had just pushed the last crumbs of pie into his mouth. 'Another?' he suggested.

'I won't say no,' said Callum, reaching into the basket. 'These are good.'

'Glad you're enjoying them. So . . . what was your role in last night's adventure?'

'My role?' Callum swallowed a chunk of pie. He thought about what had happened – how he'd gone off to pass water and how he'd ended up wetting himself when the wolfhound chased after him. He decided there was nothing there he wanted to share with anyone. 'Oh, I just helped out with things. You know . . . tethering the bait and so on. Fraser is the one who deserves all the credit.' Mentioning the goat reminded him of something. He pointed to the kid that he had tethered to a railing a short distance away, still bleating miserably. 'We need to get that wee fellow back to his master,' he said.

'I can do that for you on my way back to the inn,' offered Andrew. He winked. 'I'll even collect the deposit for you if you like. Between you and me, I think the owner was hoping that the goat wouldn't be coming back again! Mr McCloud paid out four times what it was worth!' He looked over to the gibbet where Fraser was now being lifted on to the shoulders of several burly-looking men. 'Ah, it's all kicking off now,' he said. 'I'd say Mr McCloud is going to have quite a sore head tomorrow.'

Callum was about to reply when he noticed a rider galloping into the square and recognised Michael, Colonel Chivers's coachman, his face set into a frown. He reigned his horse to a halt, looked quickly around and soon spotted Fraser being chaired around the square, whilst taking eager swigs from the stone jug. Michael urged his horse into the crowd, edging people roughly aside in his haste.

'What's the matter with him?' wondered Andrew. 'He seems to be in a big hurry.' He moved instinctively towards the action and Callum went with him, still eating his pie.

When Michael was just a short distance from Fraser, he shouted at a volume that stopped everyone in their tracks. 'Mr McCloud! The colonel sent me to find you.'

Fraser looked down from the shoulders of the men who were holding him, a puzzled expression on his face. Then he grinned and pointed towards the great hairy shape hanging from the gibbet. 'You can tell the colonel that all his troubles are over,' he said. 'There is your killer, brought down by a healthy dose of lead shot.'

Michael turned to look at the carcass for a moment, but his grim expression didn't change for an instant.

'Well, that's your wolfhound, isn't it?'

Michael nodded. 'That's him, all right,' he muttered. Then he glared at Fraser. 'There's been another one,' he said.

# 15

# UNEXPECTED

Fraser's expression went slowly from a delighted grin to a look of complete bafflement. 'Another *what*?' he muttered.

'I think you know what I'm saying,' said Michael. He glanced awkwardly around. 'Or do you need me to spell it out for you.'

'Another?' Fraser glared at him. 'But how can that be possible?' He pointed again to the dead wolfhound. 'Can't you see what's hanging from that damned gibbet?'

Michael shrugged. 'I can see it perfectly,' he said.

'Then . . . what are you blathering about?'

'It seems I *do* need to spell it out. Very well. There was another attack last night. Another of the colonel's crofters has gone missing.'

There were murmurs of dismay from the crowd. People looked fearfully at each other and started whispering intently.

Fraser looked around at them in alarm. He handed the stone jug to one of the men who was chairing him on their shoulders. 'Set me down,' he urged them. 'Now!' he added, when they were too slow in following the order. Once on his feet, he strode closer to Michael and stared up at him. 'You're sure of this?' he asked. 'There can be no mistake?'

Michael shook his head. 'Believe me, Mr McCloud, I don't like it any better than you do, but it's the truth.'

Fraser grabbed the bridle of Michael's horse. 'You're coming with me,' he announced, and before Michael could protest, he led the man's horse away from the crowd and quickly into the mouth of a narrow alleyway. Callum, still finishing off his pie, instinctively followed them and only after he had gone a few steps did he realise that Andrew was still beside him. Once Fraser had walked a decent distance along the alley, he turned back to Michael, his eyes blazing.

'What's the matter with you?' he snarled. 'Why would you say a thing like that in front of all those people?'

Michael shrugged and leaned over in his saddle. 'I'm sorry, but you rather forced me to do it. And it may be inconvenient, Mr McCloud, but it happens to be the truth.'

'And when was this supposed to have taken place?'

'We can't be sure, but we think it was in the early hours of this morning.'

Fraser shook his head. 'But . . . that cannot be! The hound you saw hanging in the square was also shot last night. Are you trying to tell me that there's more than one of these creatures?'

'I'm only telling you what I know. I've just come from the croft of a man called Peter Renton. It's the same story as the Gilmour's. Door smashed in, the place wrecked. No sign of the man who lives there.'

'Peter Renton?' It was Andrew who spoke. He moved closer to Fraser. 'He was at the Shepherd's Crook last night, drinking with some of the other crofters.' He frowned. 'I thought there was something wrong with him.'

Fraser frowned. 'How do you mean?' he asked. 'Wrong?'

'Well, it's unlike him to take a drink, for one thing. He usually only has a mug of ale on high days and holy days. But last night he was in his cups, buying whisky for him and his friends. I said to him, "Why the sudden thirst, Peter?" and he said, "You canna take it with you."'

'Anything else?'

Andrew seemed to search his memories before adding, 'Well, I seem to recall him saying something about . . . seeing which way the wind was blowing . . . and realising that he'd made a big mistake.'

Fraser pondered for a moment. 'I'm wondering perhaps if the wolfhound could have got to him first and then made its way back to the forest, where we were waiting for it,' He looked up at Michael. 'Do you have any idea what time the attack happened?'

Michael shook his head. 'It wasn't noticed until early this morning. A friend of Renton's called to the croft for some reason and found it in a state of disarray. Like I said, it was the same story as at the Gilmour's. The only difference . . .'

'Yes? Spit it out, man?'

Michael looked uncomfortable. 'The only difference was the money.'

'What money?' demanded Fraser.

'A great pile of coins set out on the doorstep of the croft. On the *outside* step, you understand, and scattered all around by whatever came in. A goodly sum, it was. It had just been left there, as though Peter was making an offering to someone.'

Fraser seemed baffled. 'It's a wonder somebody passing by didn't help themselves to it,' he said.

'But nobody wants to take it, do they?' said Callum, and the three men turned their heads to look at him. 'That's probably the 'big mistake' Mr Renton was talking about. Taking the colonel's money.' He looked up at Michael. 'Was he one of the men who helped clear the land?' he asked.

Michael nodded. 'I believe he was,' he said. 'What of it?'

'There you are, then,' said Callum. He looked at Fraser. 'You said you were looking for a pattern, didn't you? Everyone who's gone missing has—'

'Whisht!' interrupted Fraser. 'Enough of your crackpot theories.' He turned back to Andrew. 'What time did this man leave the Shepherd's Crook?'

'It was after midnight before he was done drinking. And he only left then because his friends all said they'd had enough for one night and they wanted their beds. I asked him if he would be all right walking across the moor in the dark and he said he'd done it many times over the years, why should it be a problem now, and besides, wasn't there a hunter's moon to light his way? I remember, I looked at the clock as I was locking up after him and it was twenty minutes after twelve when he set off. It would have taken him perhaps thirty or forty minutes to reach home.'

Fraser looked hopefully at Callum. 'Any idea what time I shot that wolfhound?' he asked.

'None. I don't have a timepiece. But . . . it must have been the early hours of the morning, I think. Two or three o'clock, maybe?'

'Well, there you are then! There's our answer. The hound took Renton from his croft some time after midnight and dragged him back to the forest, only to find us waiting for him. End of story.'

Michael shook his head. 'If that hound killed Renton, then where is the body? Indeed, where are *any* of the bodies? It's five people now and we haven't found a trace.'

Callum took a step closer to Fraser. 'Why can't you accept what I'm telling you?' he insisted. 'Every missing person so far has taken money from the colonel . . . and that includes Mrs Gilmour. Mr Renton must have realised that he was in danger. Why else would a poor crofter put all his money out on the step like that? He was trying to give it back.'

Michael gave a derisive laugh. 'What nonsense!' he cried. 'It would be an easier task to list the people in these parts who *haven't* taken the colonel's coin. He pays *me* a wage, doesn't he? Should I be worried?' He looked at Andrew. 'And I can only guess at the money he's put your way over the years.'

Andrew looked wounded by the remark. 'Only for perfectly respectable reasons,' he insisted. 'I certainly had no hand in clearing that woodland, if that's what you're suggesting.'

'No, of course not. But I doubt that Mrs Gilmour was handy with an axe, either,' Michael reminded him. 'If we are to believe this boy's theory then anybody who has ever accepted a single penny from the colonel is in danger.'

'We three are all in the same boat,' Fraser told him. 'We're all being paid for services rendered to the colonel. Just honest toil, nothing sinister. Surely nobody could argue with that. A man is entitled to make a living, isn't he?' He thought for a moment. 'I'm willing to bet money that now the wolfhound is dead, there'll be no more of these disappearances. My belief is that the hound has some kind of larder hidden away in the woods where he stores his victims, and where he returns at his leisure to feed upon them. No doubt somebody will stumble upon it sooner or later and a grisly sight it shall be!'

Michael frowned. 'So, you're saying—'

'I'm saying that last night, returning to his larder, the hound heard the sound of the tethered goat and found it irresistible. So, he left his first victim and along he trotted, to the place where my rifle was ready and waiting for him. Trust me, gentlemen, the reign of terror is over.' He gestured to Michael. 'You can return to Colonel Chivers and tell him that from me.'

Michael looked puzzled. 'You're not coming with me to look at the Renton croft?'

Fraser shook his head. 'What would be the point?' he asked. 'You've already told me it's the same as all the others. No, you head back to Chivers Hall and tell the colonel he can sleep easy. Everything is resolved.'

Michael seemed far from happy with the outcome, but he obligingly turned his horse around and trotted away. Fraser redirected his attention to Andrew. 'As for you, once I've reassured the people in the square that everything is fine, me and Callum will head up to the inn for a celebratory meal. I feel we've earned that much.'

Andrew seemed happy enough with the decision. 'I'll go and ensure that there's something good on the menu,' he said, and walked after Michael. 'And I'll take back that wee goat to its owner and collect your deposit,' he added, over his shoulder. He hesitated for a moment and looked back. 'I hope you're right about this,' he said, and then went on his way.

Callum looked at Fraser despairingly. 'Are you sure this is the right decision?' he asked. 'Telling everyone that the creature is dead? You can't be sure. What if you're wrong? What if the wolfhound is the one that's been killing the sheep and ... something else has been taking the people?'

'Something else meaning that damned faerie dog, I suppose?' Fraser laughed dismissively. 'Oh, that Mhairi has really turned your head, hasn't she? She'll have you believing in elves and goblins before she's through. She'll have you chanting their pagan hymns in the middle of the night!'

'Why do you insist on saying that it's all her fault?' asked Callum. 'I keep telling you there are plenty of others around here who believe in the people of the forest. She's not alone!'

'Aye, but she's the one they all look up to, isn't she? Mhairi, who knows that place like the back of her hand. You be careful, lad. She's got her hooks into you and once a female does that, there's no escape.' He walked nearer, his face grave. 'And I'll also remind you not to go shooting your mouth off about your wild theories in front of others.'

'It's not *my* theory!'

'No matter. As far as I'm concerned, our work here is done, and in a day or so we'll be heading back to Mother McCloud with a small fortune in our purses.'

Callum raised his eyebrows. 'We?' he murmured. 'Don't you mean 'you'? I don't get a wage, remember?'

'We'll have to see, won't we?' said Fraser. 'Maybe you've done enough to earn yourself a small reward.'

Callum shook his head. 'Oh, I don't want anything, thank you,' he said. 'Not unless the reward you're talking about is me being allowed to go back to my family.'

'You're easily pleased,' said Fraser. 'Who the hell would wish to return to those two fools?' He laughed unpleasantly and retraced his steps along the alley to the square, where a small crowd of villagers were waiting to talk to him. Even at this distance, it was evident that he was feeding them exactly what they wanted to hear. Callum watched as Fraser threw his arms around the shoulders of two of the men who had been chairing him and walked them away in the direction of the gibbet, talking loudly as he went. 'Fear not, gentlemen, everything is settled! It was no more than a wee misunderstanding. Now where's that jug I had before?'

Callum sighed. He couldn't help feeling that Fraser was trying to convince himself as much as anyone else. But what if he was wrong about this? What if there was something else out there?

He blinked, aware that the long sleepless night had tired him. He decided to collect Molly and ride back to the Shepherd's Crook, where his first desire was to catch up on some much-needed sleep.

# 16

# PERCHANCE TO DREAM

Callum was beginning to long for the good old days; a time when he could lie down, close his eyes and drift off into a deep, dreamless sleep. It had all been so easy back then. Exhausted from a day's toil at the McCloud's, he'd had no trouble pushing everything aside and tumbling gratefully down into darkness.

But these nights, his slumbers were a disturbing mix of dimly glimpsed images, each one more threatening than the last. He was in the forest at night, running from something that followed him on silent paws; he was crouched behind a rock next to Fraser, desperately trying to reload his employer's flintlock with hands that shook so badly, he kept dropping the lead shot into the undergrowth; he was at the Clootie Well, watching as Mhairi's face, illuminated by fireflies, gradually turned into something monstrous . . .

It was almost a relief when a hand shook him roughly awake and he found himself staring up into those familiar pale red eyes, illuminated now, not by fireflies, but by the lantern she was holding. The look on her face was one of urgency.

'What? What's wrong?' he gasped.

'I've found it,' she told him.

'Have you?' he murmured. 'That's great news. Well, I'll just get back to sleep then.'

'NO!' She was so agitated that she punched him hard on the arm, instantly dispelling any notion he might have had that she would leave him to his slumbers. 'Don't you want to know what it is I've found?'

He gazed at her blankly. 'Tell me,' he suggested.

She leant closer still and for a forlorn moment, he thought she might be thinking of kissing him again, but no such luck. 'The pattern,' she said.

'The . . . pattern,' he repeated. 'Ah, right.' A moment of silence passed before he asked, 'What pattern?'

'Didn't you say that Fraser was looking for a pattern in all this? The disappearances and everything?'

'I already told him about the wood-cutting and about people taking money from the colonel, but he just brushed it aside.'

'Yes? Well, look here. Let's see him brush this off.'

She set the lantern down on the straw – something which struck Callum as a dangerous thing to do, although he wasn't going to be the one to say it. Mhairi was unfolding a large piece of paper for him to look at. He groaned softly, got himself into a sitting position and gazed down upon it, noting that it had been written upon here and there in black ink. Each inscription seemed to consist of a cross, a date and a couple of words.

Callum blinked and waved a hand at the paper. 'What is this?' he asked.

'It's a kind of map,' she told him. 'I made it myself.'

'You can write?' he muttered. He found himself more impressed by her every day.

'Of course,' she said irritably. 'Why, can't you?'

'Not much,' he admitted. 'I can sign my name, but that's about it. I'd like to learn, but . . . well, my parents never have the money for school.'

'I'll give you some lessons,' she offered. 'Anyway, that's for later.' She pointed to a wavy line drawn near the left edge of the sheet. 'You see this? That's the edge of the Forest of Tay. And here . . .' she indicated a bold black circle a short distance to the right, '. . . is the faerie circle.'

'Ah, I see.' Callum nodded.

'Now, look.' Mhairi moved her hand a few more inches to the right. 'You see this cross? And the date? That was only a few days after the land was cleared. And you see the name?' She glanced at him apologetically and read it aloud for him. 'Hugh McCarron,' she said. 'The first tenant to disappear and, as you can see, he was the one who lived closest to the forest.'

Callum frowned. 'And he helped with the wood clearing?'

'Correct.' Mhairi leant back a little and indicated the rest of the crosses and names. Callum could see that each successive cross, though irregularly spaced – some higher, some lower on the paper – all moved further and further to the right.

'So, you're saying that each time the creature comes out of the forest . . .'

'He moves closer and closer to *this*.' She indicated another big cross close to the right-hand side of the sheet.

'What's that?' he asked.

'That is Chivers Hall,' said Mhairi. 'And I believe it is the beast's final destination. I think that once it's finished gathering up the monkeys, it'll call for the organ grinder.' She slid her finger back to the left again and showed him where two crosses sat right next to each other. 'The Gilmours,' she told him. 'Hamish and his poor wife, Shona. She surely didn't deserve her fate. She was only trying to fend for her bairns and now look at them! Orphans, both.'

'We don't know for sure that she's dead,' Callum reminded her.

'What, you think she's being held captive somewhere?' She shook her head. 'I very much doubt it. I don't think that creature takes any prisoners.' Again, she moved her index finger a short distance to the right. 'Here's the home of the most recent victim,' she said. 'Peter Renton. Now, I've thought long and hard to see if I could come up with anyone else from round these parts who helped clear the land around that damned circle, but it seems to me that everyone else who worked on it was brought in from outside the area.'

Callum studied the map for a moment. 'But,' he said. 'There's one more cross between Mr Renton and the hall, so who . . .?'

Mhairi let out a deep sigh and Callum glanced up at her. He was shocked and surprised to see two wet trails coursing down her cheeks. They dripped from her chin and made two dark splashes on the paper.

'Oh Mhairi, you don't think . . .?'

She nodded. 'The Shepherd's Crook,' she said. 'I think we're next.'

There was a long silence, broken only by the sound of Mhairi's sobs. Callum reached out an arm and put it gently around her shoulders.

'Here now,' he murmured. 'Don't take on so. You've done nothing wrong.'

'No, I haven't. But what about Andrew? He has taken the

colonel's shilling many a time. And I happen to know that he helped recruit the men for that forest clearance.'

'Surely not!'

'It's true. The colonel's carriage called here only a few days before the work started and he and Andrew spent ages in the back room talking something over. Andrew wouldn't have worked for nothing, he never does.'

'But, if he didn't pick up an axe, then surely . . .'

'Mrs Gilmour didn't pick one up either,' snarled Mhairi. She shook her head. 'Don't you see? Andrew's hands are tainted with the colonel's blood money, like all the others. I tried telling him what he needed to do. I said he should go to the colonel and give him back every penny he's been given by that man, right from the very beginning, but he just laughed at me! He asked me where I supposed he should start.'

'And . . .' Callum tapped the sheet of paper. 'Have you shown him this?'

'Not yet. I only just finished working it out and I wanted to get your thoughts on it.'

'My thoughts?' Callum grimaced. 'I hope you're wrong, Mhairi, but written out like that, it looks pretty convincing.'

Mhairi dashed at her eyes with the sleeve of her dress. 'I was hoping that perhaps you could talk to Mr McCloud. Tell him to be ready for when the creature . . . the real one, comes calling. Maybe the two of you could stand guard by the front door every night and wait for it.'

Callum didn't know what to say to her. 'You think he'd listen to me?' he asked her. 'Let me tell you about Fraser McCloud. He'll be over in his room, right now, sleeping off all the drink he poured into himself earlier. He's no reason to have nightmares tonight. He believes he's killed the wolf or the *Cù Sìth*, or whatever the hell it is. He thinks his work is done. And don't even dream that he'll consider giving back any of the money he's been paid.'

'Then what are we to do?' cried Mhairi. 'We can't just sit around and wait for it to happen!'

Callum thought for a moment, then reached out and carefully folded up the map. He tucked it into the inside pocket of his jacket. 'I'll show this to Fraser first thing tomorrow,' he promised her. 'I'll explain it all to him, just as you've explained it to me. He'll surely see that this is the pattern he's been looking for. He'll *have* to.'

Mhairi studied him mournfully. 'And if he doesn't believe you?'

Callum gazed at her. He considered for a moment and then said again, 'I'll talk to him.'

'Thank you.' She leant forward and kissed him gently on the cheek. 'And now, I have to go,' she said. 'There's always work to do.'

'So late?' he murmured. 'Can't you stay a while?'

'I'm afraid not.'

He tried not to look disappointed. 'I'll see you tomorrow then,' he murmured.

'Aye.' She kissed him lightly on the lips and then picking up the lantern, she scrambled past him and went down the ladder at speed. He leant closer to the hatch and looked down at her, illuminated by the pool of light from the lantern. She got down on to the ground and turned to leave. The light fell briefly on the figure of old Tam, spread out on his straw palette, his head back. His mouth was open as usual but oddly, so were his eyes. Mhairi hesitated a moment and gazed down at him. Then she reached out a foot and gingerly prodded the old man with the toe of her boot.

'Oh,' she said.

Callum gazed down at her. 'Something wrong?' he whispered.

She looked back up at him, her face even paler than usual. 'I think he's dead,' she murmured.

'Are you joking?'

'I'm afraid not.' She frowned. 'It's odd. He was sleeping normally when I came by him, just now.'

Callum glared down at her, remembering what Mhairi had said to Tam, only last night. That he was doomed. That he had only one more day left to live.

Mhairi was gazing back at him, her expression blank. And then she seemed to realise what was on his mind. 'Oh,' she murmured. 'You don't think . . . you don't think that I had anything to do with this, do you?'

He had to say what was on his mind. 'Mhairi, you *cursed* him. I was there, I heard you say it.'

'Aye, but I was only joking. Just putting the fear into him. I certainly didn't mean . . .'

He continued to look at her, his expression hard. 'Tell me the truth,' he whispered. 'Did you kill Tam?'

She opened her mouth to reply but the answer never came.

Instead, they both jumped as a noise came from across the courtyard – a loud crash, as though something solid had just been smashed to pieces. Mhairi's eyes widened in realisation. 'Oh no!' she gasped. 'Oh, please, no!' She turned and ran out of the stable, taking the lantern with her. Then Callum was blundering down the ladder in pursuit. He tripped on one of the last rungs and went down in a sprawl, landing on top of Tam's outstretched body, the impact squeezing a last breath out of him.

For an instant, the old man's blind eyes seemed to stare straight into his and the reek of his tobacco-cured lungs filled Callum's nostrils. He gave a grunt of disgust, rolled aside and got himself upright. Outside, across the courtyard, the noise continued. It sounded like the gates of hell were opening wide.

Callum snatched in a breath and ran through the open door of the stable.

# 17

# NEXT

Callum raced across the cobbled courtyard, his heart hammering in his chest. He was dimly aware of Mhairi running frantically ahead of him towards the inn's main entrance. As she drew close to the steps, she came to an abrupt halt and stood there, staring at the doorway in disbelief. Callum came up alongside her and he too, stopped in his tracks. He could not prevent himself from letting out a horrified gasp. The solid wooden doors were gone, smashed into heaps of matchwood as though they'd been struck by a prodigious force. It was the same story as at the Gilmours', except these doors had been four times the size. Callum asked himself what kind of creature could have done so much damage.

'I pulled them shut when I came out to the stable,' cried Mhairi. 'I didn't want to wake anyone. I . . . couldn't know that it would come so soon . . .'

She broke off at the sound of a woman's scream from somewhere within the inn and she ran up the steps and into the main room, with Callum close on her heels. The room was dark but the dull glow from the dying embers of the log fire was enough to show that the place had been wrecked; tables and chairs overturned, pots and mugs smashed to pieces. Again, the woman's scream came from upstairs, sounding more urgent now, more frantic. *Mrs Blantyre?* wondered Callum.

Mhairi crossed the room to the doorway at the back and turned right into the corridor beyond. She led Callum along a narrow hallway, which opened out at the foot of a massive staircase. Looking up, Callum could see a scene of complete confusion up on the first-floor landing. Various people – some half-dressed, some still in their nightshirts – were milling around in total confusion, asking each other urgent questions, somebody holding up a lit candle to try and illuminate the scene. A heavyset woman in a nightgown, her red hair tied in rags, came blundering down the staircase, screaming incoherently as she approached. Mhairi intercepted her halfway up and grabbed her by the wrist.

'Mrs Blantyre!' she cried, and the woman stared at her, wide-eyed, as if she didn't know who was speaking to her. She pointed a shaking finger back up the stairs. 'It ran right by me!' she gasped. 'The size of it! And its eyes . . . its horrible red eyes!'

'Where's Andrew?' asked Mhairi, clearly making a supreme effort to keep calm. 'Did you see him?'

'He's in his room I think . . . he . . .' She stopped speaking as a sound came from upstairs – a hideous, echoing howl – horribly loud and enough to stun the crowd on the landing into shocked silence. Everyone listened in mute horror. Then came the yelling of a man's voice.

'No!' it screamed. 'No, please. I've done nothing! I'm innocent!'

Callum thought he recognised Andrew's voice, though it was so shrill, it was hard to be sure. Mhairi let go of Mrs Blantyre and pounded up to the landing, pushing her way past an assortment of guests who were descending with all haste. Mrs Blantyre went back to screaming as loud as she could. She reached ground level and ran for the main room.

Callum followed Mhairi, telling himself that whatever happened he needed to stick close to her; that she too might be in danger. A burly, half-dressed guest blundered into him, nearly knocking him headlong over the bannister rail, but he clung grimly on until the man had gone past and then continued upwards to the landing. He caught a glimpse of Mhairi as she raced around a corner and he tried to follow her, but his path was obstructed as a bedroom door swung open, slamming into him and nearly knocking him off his feet. A figure in a long white nightshirt stepped out from behind the open door and gazed at Callum in bleary-eyed astonishment.

For a moment, Callum barely recognised Fraser. Still addled by drink and wearing a nightshirt that wouldn't have looked out of place on Mother McCloud, he presented a foolish spectacle. In different circumstances, it might have made Callum laugh, but this wasn't funny. This wasn't funny at all.

'What in the name of Hades' flames is going on here?' bellowed Fraser, and Callum snatched a few precious moments to fling a rebuke at him.

'What do you suppose is happening?' he snarled. 'The creature is here. You know, the one you claim to have killed?'

Fraser stared back at him, as though not understanding. 'But . . . that cannot be,' he whispered. 'You saw it die. You saw it hanging from that gibbet.'

'Not *that* creature,' Callum assured him. 'The other one. The *real* one.'

Up on the next floor, Andrew's pleas dissolved into another

scream of pure terror. Fraser seemed to snap suddenly out of his trance and he lurched back into his room. 'My rifle,' he muttered.

'Aye, get your damned rifle!' shouted Callum, realising he would probably pay for his recklessness later but for now, too pressed to care. 'For all the good it will do!'

He ran on along the landing and turned right where another flight of stairs led up to the second floor. Halfway along the next landing, he saw Mhairi. She was kneeling in front of a smashed door, her hands clasped in front of her as if in prayer.

'Please spare him,' she was saying, addressing something in the darkened room, something that Callum could not yet see. 'Please, I beg you. He'll give the money back, every penny. I'll make sure of it.'

Callum slowed his pace and approached cautiously until he was standing right behind Mhairi and was able to look into the room. The only light in there came through a chink in the curtained windows. The beam illuminated Andrew, who was also kneeling. There was a deep cut on his forehead from which blood was running profusely, turning his face into a mask of horror. He was staring wide-eyed at something that was crouched in front of him – something huge – a great sinewy beast, its powerful shoulders hunched, its huge paws splayed on the floorboards. A low rumbling growl was coming from it; a sound so low that the entire room seemed to vibrate. Andrew's whole body shook with fear. 'No,' he moaned. 'No.'

'PLEASE!' screamed Mhairi. 'You don't have to take him. He's a good man. He's done nobody any harm.'

Callum thought about entering the room, though he didn't have the first idea what he might do when he got there, but then he heard footsteps thudding along the landing. Looking to his left, he saw Fraser racing towards him, still dressed in his nightshirt, his flintlock at his side. He saw Callum and Mhairi at the door and, pushing Callum roughly aside, he swung the rifle into position over Mhairi's shoulder to draw aim at whatever was crouched in front of Andrew.

'Now I have you,' Callum heard him say.

There was a moment of silence when everything froze in time. And then it all happened at once: the roar of the gun in the enclosed space, the blinding flash of the powder as it caught fire, the fierce blast of smoke that hit Callum's eyes, making them sting. He held his breath, hardly daring to hope. In the room, the creature was in motion, lunging towards Andrew. The landlord had time for one last terrified squeal before the creature's huge jaws fastened around his throat and then bore him upwards, backwards, towards the curtained window. Callum shouted something, he didn't know what. The curtains tore from their fastenings, enclosing the beast and Andrew's struggling body. The glass behind them shattered, the stout window frames snapping like twigs, and the beast and its victim broke through and dropped to the courtyard far below.

'FATHER!' screamed Mhairi, and Callum looked at her dumbstruck, realising that this was the first time he had ever heard her call Andrew that. Beside Callum, Fraser shouted an oath and ran into the room, to peer out of the shattered window. For a moment, he seemed turned to stone – but then he spun around, dropping the rifle and raced back towards the door.

'The pistol!' he gasped as he blundered by and then he was running barefoot along the landing, but Callum already knew there was no hope of stopping this beast with a shot from a pistol and, what was worse, there was no hope for Andrew.

Mhairi struggled to her feet and stumbled into the room. Callum went after her. They reached the window and stared down on to the moonlit courtyard. There was the tangle of fabric that had been the curtains, discarded on the cobbles like some huge cocoon and, up by the stables, a dark shape was racing out towards the moor, carrying what looked like a broken doll in its jaws. Just then, Fraser ran into view from below. He stumbled down the steps to the level ground, raising the pistol to fire again. He unleashed a shot, the flash of light briefly illuminating him, but even if he'd been close enough to hit the creature, he couldn't have hoped to kill it. Fraser stood for a moment, staring towards the moor as though half expecting the thing to come back at him – but it had vanished into the same darkness that it had emerged from. Fraser hung his head, his shoulders slumped and he turned dejectedly back towards the broken doorway of the inn.

A sound escaped from Mhairi – a low, keening groan of despair.

'I begged him to give the money back,' she whispered, 'I pleaded with him. But he wouldn't listen. Why doesn't anybody ever listen?'

She shook her head and Callum could see the tears streaming down her face. He moved closer and put his arms around her, pulling her close. She sobbed against his chest like a child and he heard her say something but couldn't make it out, so he relaxed his hold and let her pull away a little. She raised her face to look imploringly up at him.

'I didn't kill Old Tam,' she whispered. 'I promise you I didn't. I just wanted to scare him. You do believe me, don't you?'

He stared at her. 'Of course,' he said, and pulled her close again. But he knew in his heart that he still wasn't sure about it; that he would probably never be certain, as long as he lived.

# 18

# A MAN'S WORD

The morning dawned, grey and drizzly, turbulent clouds blocking the sun as if trying to suffocate it. Callum left Mhairi asleep in Andrew's bed and went downstairs to look for Fraser. The inn was eerily deserted. There was no sign of any guests or staff, and, in the cold light of day, it was all too easy to see the devastation wrought by the *Cù Sìth*. Even the walls bore the violent signs of the creature's passing – claw marks gouged deep into whitewashed plaster.

Callum eventually found Fraser amidst the wreckage of the main room. He had managed to find a relatively unscathed table and chair and was sitting alone, sipping at a mug of hot coffee. He looked dreadful, Callum thought, pale-faced and unshaven, his eyes rimmed red from lack of sleep. He glanced up as Callum came into the room and, after a moment's thought, he filled a second mug from a metal pot, then gestured to Callum to come and join him.

Callum looked around the room and in a far corner, spotted a chair that still appeared to have four legs that might just hold his weight. He dragged it across to the table and sat down opposite his employer. He wouldn't have thought it possible, but he actually felt sorry for Fraser right now. All of that cocksure arrogance had been driven right out of him. Now he just looked rumpled and anxious.

'I couldn't have known,' he said quietly. 'How could I have realised there was more than one of those things?'

Callum just shrugged his shoulders and took a sip of the coffee, which was strong and very, very bitter. He grimaced.

'Couldn't find any sugar,' muttered Fraser. 'It was a small miracle I located the coffee.' He glanced around. 'Not a soul in the place, now. They've all gone, even Mrs Blantyre. Frightened off by that damned creature.'

Callum put down his mug and fixed Fraser with a look. 'Damned is the right word,' he said. 'You saw what was in Andrew's room. You can't pretend any more that it's just some overgrown hound.'

Fraser scowled. 'It was dark in there,' he countered. 'I never got a clear look at it . . .'

Callum raised his eyebrows.

'You put a shot into it at point blank range,' he reminded Fraser. 'It didn't even slow it down. Now, try and tell me again that it's just a hunting dog gone wild.'

Fraser let out a sigh. 'Yes, I saw something that was like no creature I've ever seen before, I'll grant you that. But I can't be sure I hit it. I think I did, but . . .' He took another gulp of his coffee. 'How is the girl?' he asked.

'How you'd expect her to be,' said Callum. 'She cried the entire night long and didn't get to sleep until a few minutes ago.' He shook his head. 'Are you surprised? She saw her father slaughtered, right in front of her eyes. It's a wonder she hasn't gone mad.'

'Not her real father, from what I've heard.'

'Does it matter? Andrew is the one who raised her; it's the same thing.'

'That's a matter of opinion,' said Fraser quietly, and Callum found that his newly discovered sympathy for the man was already starting to wear thin. He remembered what had happened last night and withdrew the folded sheet of paper from his jacket. He set it down on the table. Fraser studied it suspiciously.

'What's this?' he asked.

'It's a map that Mhairi made. We were looking at it last night, when . . . when the visitor arrived. It's the pattern you were looking for.' Callum unfolded the map and gave Fraser a breakdown of what Mhairi had told him, pointing out each location in turn. 'She knew the Shepherd's Crook was next,' he said. 'But she didn't realise it would be so soon.'

Fraser rubbed his stubbled chin. 'And she's certain that Chivers Hall is the only place left?' he muttered.

'Aye. She couldn't think of anyone else in these parts who might be a target.' He looked at Fraser. 'So, what are we going to do?'

Fraser appeared to ponder the matter for a few moments. 'We go there, before it gets dark,' he said at last.

'We go where?' Callum stared at him. 'To Chivers Hall?'

'Of course. Where else?'

'And why exactly would we do that?'

'So we'll be ready for the beast when it arrives.'

Callum actually gasped, such was his disbelief. 'But that doesn't make any sense,' he protested. 'We already know that your bullets have no effect on that thing, so . . .'

'I've been thinking about that,' reasoned Fraser. 'It might simply be a matter of aim. That was a hurried shot I made last night. I aimed into its flank. But a well-placed bullet right between the creature's eyes, that would be a different proposition.'

'No, Fraser, listen to me. I don't understand. Why would you go to Chivers Hall? You'd be signing your own death warrant. In your place, I'd be riding for home, right now. At a gallop. Perhaps if we can get far enough away from that creature, we'll be able to outrun it. We could . . .'

But Fraser had got to his feet, his expression one of outrage. 'Run from it?' he snapped. 'Run? And shirk my responsibilities?'

'What responsi—'

'I made an arrangement with the colonel, did I not?' interrupted Fraser. 'I promised him I would take care of his problem. I thought I'd succeeded in that endeavour, but I was wrong. So I need to correct that mistake. A man's word is his bond, don't you know that? I shook the colonel's hand, for God's sake. Now you're suggesting I should run like a coward with my tail between my legs!'

'But please, think about it for a moment. You didn't have the full story when you shook his hand. He fed you a pack of half-truths. Do you suppose *he* acted honourably?'

'That's not the point. If I run away from this, I'd have to live with it for the rest of my life.'

'At least you'd have some life left to live,' Callum snapped. He thought for a moment. 'There's something else I should have told you,' he added. 'About your shirt.'

'My shirt?' Fraser was clearly mystified.

'Aye. The white one. You noticed it was gone the day we arrived here?'

'What of it?'

Callum wasn't sure how his next words would be taken. 'You . . . also remember when we were looking for the Gilmour's Croft? The old woman you sent me to ask directions of?'

Fraser scowled. 'The one you said sang at you?'

'Yes, her. She, well, she was washing a shirt in the river. A white shirt. There was . . . there was blood coming out of it.'

'Is this supposed to mean something to me?' Fraser asked him. 'Because I have to tell you, you sound like you're rambling.'

'She was the Washer at the Ford. She's famous! She cleanses the clothes of those who are soon to die. The shirt was just like the one you lost.'

There was a silence while the two of them stared at each other. Then Fraser leant back his head and laughed derisively. 'Oh, now I've heard everything!' he bellowed. 'The Washer at the Ford! Of course! How silly of me not to recognise her. And how, pray tell me, did she manage to get her hands on my best shirt? Did she go through my pack when I wasn't looking?'

Callum made a helpless gesture. 'I don't know,' he said. 'She must have used some kind of magic. But . . .'

'Mhairi's done it, hasn't she?' said Fraser, shaking his head. 'The clever wee minx. She's managed to convert you to her pagan ways – lock, stock and barrel. She's got you believing every stupid thing she comes up with. What next, I wonder? Ghosts? Hobgoblins? Dragons?'

Callum was rapidly beginning to lose his temper. 'What do I have to do to convince you?' he cried. 'How much evidence do you need? If you go to Chivers Hall, that will be the end of you. And don't say I haven't warned you.'

Fraser lifted a hand and stepped forward, as though intending to knock Callum out of his chair, but at the last moment, he lowered his arm. 'You're distraught,' he said. 'I need to make allowances for that.' He coughed and paced restlessly around for a moment. Then he stopped. 'You can prepare the horses, ready to leave for the hall . . . and you can take a few moments to say goodbye to your. . . friend, Mhairi.'

Callum glowered at Fraser. 'You're asking me to go with you?' he gasped.

'I'm not asking,' Fraser corrected him. 'I'm *telling* you. The last time I checked, you still worked for me, and you'll do as you're told.'

'But that's not fair! You can't make me do it.'

'Oh, can't I?' Fraser gave him a knowing look. 'Well, of course, since your father can't pay off his debt . . . and as you're not ready to step up to the mark . . . I suppose there's always that fine-looking mother of yours. Perhaps *she'd* be willing to work for me to pay off her husband's debt.'

Callum swallowed hard. Now Fraser was back to where he'd been before, provoking Callum's hatred.

'I'll go with you,' he said tonelessly.

'Excellent. Get to it then! I fulfil all my obligations and I expect you to do the same. Don't forget, it was your father's idiocy that bound you over to me in the first place. Now, hurry up, the day's already advancing, and we have work to do. *Men's* work. I'm going up to pack my bags. Be ready to leave in fifteen minutes.'

And with that, he strode out of the room. Callum sat where he was, gazing into the dregs of his mug of coffee. All he saw in there was darkness. He let out a long sigh, got up from the table and followed Fraser reluctantly out of the room.

He had expected to find Mhairi still asleep, but she was out of bed and gazing through the smashed window at the distant sweep of moor, skulking under the billowing piles of ash grey cloud.

Callum moved closer. 'I came to . . .'

'. . . say goodbye,' she finished, without turning around.

He smiled ruefully. 'For once, I'd like to say something you aren't expecting,' he said. 'That would be nice.'

'Do you really have to go with him?' she asked. 'He can't make you.'

Callum frowned. 'I'm afraid he can,' he said.

'I expect you're going to Chivers Hall?'

Callum nodded.

'But why? It doesn't make any kind of sense.'

Callum couldn't agree more. 'Fraser is afraid of being called a coward,' he explained. 'That's the kind of sense he understands.'

'But he's perfectly happy to be called an idiot?' She turned from the window, reaching into the pocket of her skirt as she did so. 'Here,' she said, and placed something into his hand.

He looked down in surprise at the brightly painted lead soldier. 'Wee Davie,' he murmured.

'He'll keep you safe,' she assured him. 'Until I see you again.'

'I wouldn't hold your breath,' he murmured. 'But, thank you.' He slipped the soldier into his own pocket. 'What will you do now?' he asked her.

She shrugged her narrow shoulders. 'Me? Oh, I dare say I'll be all right. The inn will come to me, of course. Andrew always told me it would be mine when he was gone. But I somehow thought he'd go gently in his old age. Not the way he did.' She threw a glance at the ruined window. 'I'll get the old place fixed up in time. The customers will return and so will the staff. And I'll be Mistress Mhairi of the Shepherd's Crook.' She looked at Callum, her pale red eyes weirdly alluring under her long lashes. 'And what about you?' she asked him. 'What will happen to poor Callum?'

He grimaced. 'I don't know,' he admitted. 'I made a wish at the Clootie Well. I hope it comes good for me.'

'I've a feeling it will,' she assured him. 'But here's something to keep you going in the meantime.' She reached up and kissed him gently on the lips, holding her mouth to his for a few tantalising moments.

From the landing below, Fraser's voice sounded an urgent warning.

'Don't be taking all day, boy! You've those horses to attend to.'

Callum and Mhairi moved apart.

'Hark! Your master is calling you,' murmured Mhairi, with the ghost of a smile. 'Take care out there.'

He nodded and patted his pocket. 'Wee Davie will keep me safe,' he told her. Then he turned and walked out of the room.

# 19
# A CHANGE OF HEART

Once again, they were riding across the moor and this time Mhairi wasn't there to act as their guide – but Fraser seemed to know the way well enough. He rode a short distance ahead, while Callum trailed dejectedly along behind him, his shoulders slumped, his head bowed. It felt suspiciously like he was riding towards his doom, and it crossed his mind that he could so easily turn Molly around and gallop away from there. By the time Fraser noticed what was happening, Callum would already have a head start and he could just keep going, moving south, until he'd left his employer far behind . . .

He even pictured himself doing it; kicking his heels into Molly's flanks and urging her into a gallop, and yet, somehow, he just couldn't bring himself to. It would feel too much like an act of cowardice, and he knew that Fraser would despise him for it. For some reason he couldn't quite fathom, it mattered what Fraser thought of him. And whatever his opinion of his employer, he had to admit that Fraser was showing exceptional courage by sticking to his arrangement with Colonel Chivers. And, in a strange way, that was something to be admired.

They were still a good distance from the hall when they

saw three horsemen riding urgently towards them.

'Hello, who's this?' muttered Fraser. He brought Mags to a halt and waited for the men to approach. As they drew nearer, Callum recognised Michael, the colonel's coachman and, riding behind him, the two burly gatekeepers from Chivers Hall. The three men rode up close and then reined their horses to a standstill. They sat there, looking rather shame-faced, Callum thought, as though they'd been caught doing something wrong.

'Where are you gentlemen off to in such a hurry?' Fraser asked them.

Michael shrugged his shoulders. 'Not sure yet,' he muttered. 'Just . . . somewhere else. Somewhere *safe*.' He managed to meet Fraser's gaze. 'We heard what happened at the Shepherd's Crook last night. I thought to myself, Michael, the writing's on the wall. If Andrew Sessions can fall to that creature, then so can I. So, I think . . .' He glanced back at his companions. '*We* think, it's time to look for other employment; the further from this place, the better.'

Fraser glared at Michael's companions. 'You too?' he muttered. 'The bold gatekeepers? I thought you were supposed to be fearless.'

The men sneered, but said nothing.

Fraser turned his attention back to Michael. 'And where's the colonel now?' he asked.

'Back at the hall, of course. Trying to carry on as normal. Look, it's not just us, you know. Everyone's leaving. The cook, the housekeeper, the servants - even Declan. Bad news travels fast. The rats are fleeing the sinking ship.'

'And you're joining them,' said Fraser, his voice thick with contempt. 'Leaving the old man to his fate.'

'It's of his own choosing,' protested Michael.

'Really?'

'Yes, really. I offered to take him anywhere he wanted to go. Told him I'd get the coach and drive him there. "You could be fifty miles from here by nightfall," I said. But he wouldn't hear of it. After everything that's happened, he still insists it's all superstitious nonsense. I told him, I used to think the same way, but *now* . . . we can't just try and carry on as normal.' Michael shook his head. 'I don't know if the man is just stubborn or if he thinks he knows better than everybody else. At any rate, he's adamant he's not leaving. Says they'll have to carry him out in a pine box.'

'He offered us extra money to stay,' added one of the gatekeepers. 'Said we could name our price. It was tempting, for sure. But there isn't enough coin in the world to persuade me to spend another night in that place. Riches are of no great use if you're not alive to spend them.'

Fraser grunted. 'I see. Well, happy travels, gentlemen,' he muttered. 'I hope you find yourselves better situations.' He gathered up his reins, ready to leave.

Michael stared at him in disbelief. 'You're not going to the hall, are you?'

Fraser nodded. 'I am,' he said.

'Don't be a fool, man. What's the point?'

'The point is I made an agreement with the colonel and, unlike you, I intend to see it through to the bitter end.'

'But you've also taken his coin. You'll be in danger.'

Fraser seemed to consider this for a moment. 'If that's the case, then so be it,' he said. 'I was happy enough to take the money when it was offered. I should be ready to accept the consequences.' He started to ride on, but Michael reached out a hand and grabbed Mags's bridle. 'At least let the boy come with us,' he said. 'There's no sense in taking him into such a situation. He's just a youngster, he has his whole life ahead of him.'

Fraser frowned. He turned his head to look at Callum. 'You want to go with them?' he asked. 'You can if you wish. It's your choice.'

Callum stared at Fraser in surprise. He opened his mouth to say 'yes', but oddly, frustratingly, he couldn't seem to shape that single word. It stuck in his throat like an obstinate morsel of food. 'I . . . I . . .' He looked at Michael and his two companions, noting their sheepish expressions, the way they couldn't quite look him in the eye. He turned back to Fraser, who was still watching him, his own face impassive. He told himself that at least Fraser had some kind of nobility about him, some sense of honour. And as for Michael and the gatekeepers, he wouldn't trust them for a moment.

'I'll go with you to the hall,' said Callum, and could hardly believe that he'd said it. What was wrong with him? Had he lost his mind?

But then, there was a rare occurrence. A grateful smile spread itself across Fraser's face, making him look quite unlike himself. 'Good lad,' he said. He leant forward in his saddle, pushed Michael's hand roughly away from Mags's bridle and urged her onward. Callum followed.

'You wee fool,' he heard Michael snarl. 'You realise you're following that man to your death, don't you? And for what? Some stupid notion of honour?'

'At least he's not running scared,' said Fraser, without looking back. 'And he's showing a lot more courage than you are.'

The two of them rode on for some distance in silence, but then

Callum noticed how Fraser slowed his mount a little until the two of them were riding along side-by-side. After what seemed an age, Fraser spoke.

'Thank you,' he said. 'I appreciate your loyalty.'

Callum couldn't help but stare. He had never heard Fraser say these words to him before. It felt decidedly odd. 'No problem,' he murmured. 'It just seemed like the right thing to do.'

'You know, you and I have more in common than you might think.'

Callum looked at him in surprise. 'How's that?' he asked.

'Well, for one thing we both had unsuitable fathers. My old man died when I was around your age. But he was much like yours.'

'He played cards?'

'Not so much that, no, but . . . he drank. And when he drank, he could be very handy with his fists. But, like many drunks, he died young, and I was left to look after my mother. It made me . . .' He seemed to search for the right words. '. . . ruthless, I suppose. But what I said about your mother, earlier. That I would make her work for me? That was just talk. I would never do that.'

Callum looked at him in surprise. "Oh?' he said. 'Then why say it?'

Fraser shrugged. 'I'm not sure. I suppose I wanted to bend you to my will. And, I'll be honest with you, I didn't relish the idea of facing that beast on my own.' Callum felt shocked by this confession. Fraser had told Callum more in the past two minutes than he had in all the time he'd worked for the man.

'Are you saying you're afraid?'

'I'd be crazy not to be. You saw that thing in Andrew's room last night. I'm willing to guess it put the fear into you.'

'Yes, of course. But you . . . I thought you weren't afraid of anything.'

Fraser gave a bitter little laugh. 'Well, that only goes to show,' he said. 'I've made an art of keeping my hand hidden. Perhaps that's why I'm a good card player. But listen, if we are lucky enough to come through this alive, I will consider your debt fully repaid. I'll let you return to your parents.'

Callum couldn't prevent his jaw from dropping open. 'You . . . you really mean it?'

Fraser looked slightly annoyed. 'You should know by now, lad, I do not make false promises. The matter is settled. Now, hush up, before I change my mind.'

He nodded towards a distant shape. Chivers Hall was gradually coming into focus on the horizon. 'Well, there's our destination,' he said. 'Let's see what's to be done.'

He urged Mags into a canter and, after a few moments' hesitation, Callum went after him.

*\*\*\**

The massive gates of the hall were closed but, when tried, proved to be unlocked. Fraser climbed down to swing one of the gates open, the rusting metal hinges letting out an eerie creak. He remounted Mags and led Callum along the drive towards the house.

The place appeared to be deserted but as they neared the main door, it opened, and Colonel Chivers stepped out on to the front steps. Despite the lateness of the hour, he was still wearing an embroidered dressing gown and silk slippers. He looked tired, Callum thought, and older than before, as though the last few nights had put years on him. He was unshaven and without his wig, grey wisps of hair stuck alarmingly up from his bony skull. He studied the two visitors suspiciously.

'Mr McCloud,' he said. 'Come to take your leave, I suppose, like all the others. No doubt you'll be wanting the balance of your payment?'

Fraser shook his head. 'The job's not finished yet,' he said. 'You can give me the rest of the money when it is.'

The colonel seemed taken aback at this. 'I must say, I'm pleasantly surprised,' he said. 'I've spent the morning bidding goodbye to so many people, I barely know what day of the week it is. People I trusted, people I've supported over the years. Every one of them walked out of the door without so much as a glance back at me. And all of them are convinced of the existence of this . . . supernatural creature.' He sneered. 'Now I have the irksome task of bringing in new servants from outside the area.'

'Like you did with me,' said Fraser coldly.

The colonel didn't pass comment on that.

'We passed Michael on the way,' added Fraser. 'He told us he'd offered to take you away from here.'

Colonel Chivers shrugged. 'Yes, and I told him I had no intention of leaving. This is Chivers Hall, for goodness' sake! My family home. I don't abandon it simply because some superstitious locals believe in a ridiculous curse. Michael has allowed himself to be influenced by them, but I am made of sterner stuff than that.' He frowned. 'So, if I am to understand this correctly, you hunted down Chaser and killed him, yes?'

'I did,' agreed Fraser. 'His body still hangs from the gibbet in the village square, if you'd like proof. I had supposed his death would end the matter. But then, late last night . . .'

'Andrew Sessions.' The colonel nodded. 'Yes, I heard about it. He was a decent man, I'm sorry to hear of his passing.' The colonel looked puzzled. 'And I'm told this creature actually made its way into the inn?'

'Yes. Smashed down an oak door like it was made of paper. Went inside and wrecked the place.'

'So, if it wasn't Chaser, then . . . what was it?'

Fraser frowned. 'That's a very good question. I saw the beast with my own eyes . . . I even fired a shot into it, but it had no effect whatsoever.' He shook his head. 'But trust me, Colonel, when I first came here I believed the same as you. That it was just a fanciful notion, some fairy tale concocted by people with too much time on their hands and overactive imaginations. But what I saw last night . . .' He frowned. 'That was no ordinary beast.'

The colonel chuckled. 'And you were sober, were you?'

'Not exactly. But Callum was, and he saw it too.'

The colonel turned his gaze to Callum. 'What did you see?' he asked.

'A beast the size of a bear,' said Callum. 'It picked up Andrew Sessions by his neck and carried him away like a doll. It leapt right through an upstairs window and took him off across the moor . . .'

But the colonel was sniggering now and Callum felt his cheeks burn.

'The boy's telling you the truth,' insisted Fraser. 'We both saw it. And yes, I know how it sounds. But here's the thing, Colonel. Everything seems to point to the fact that this beast, whatever it is, wherever it comes from, has been making its way towards you.'

'Towards *me*. I'm honoured!' The colonel chuckled. 'Yes, well, that is pretty much what Michael said. That he thought

I was the final target because of the woodland I cleared. But if I start to believe in such twaddle, what next, Mr McCloud? You tell me that. Do we look in the face of science and logic and say that all the advances we've made over this century have been wrong? That the stuff of fable still holds sway?'

Fraser shrugged. 'I cannot tell you what to believe,' he said 'All I know is this. I think the creature will come after you – soon – possibly tonight. Now, you have a simple choice, sir. You can climb aboard a good horse and ride as far away from here as you can . . . or we can arm ourselves and wait for the creature to arrive.'

'I've already told you, I'm not leaving. It's as simple as that.'

'Very well. In that case, we'd best prepare.' Fraser looked slowly around the grounds. 'Am I correct in believing this high stone wall encloses the hall on all four sides?' he asked.

'It does indeed.'

'Well then, assuming this devil dog cannot leap higher than twenty feet, it will have to come through the main gate.' He pointed back along the drive. 'So, the first thing we need to do is to secure that with as many locks and chains as we can lay our hands on.'

'I believe there are plenty in the stables,' said the colonel. 'Feel free to use them. But there's no four-legged creature on God's earth that can force its way through *those* gates. They've stood for centuries.'

Fraser frowned. 'Then let's hope they stand for centuries more,' he muttered. 'But what I saw of the remains of the solid oak door of the Shepherd's Crook does not fill me with much confidence on that score. And may I ask, Colonel, do you have any weapons here?'

The colonel smiled coldly. 'I have many,' he said. 'As you may have heard, my hunting parties are grand affairs. There are rifles and pistols aplenty – plus enough ammunition to supply a small army.'

Good.' Fraser nodded. 'Then, with your permission, my intention is to load up every weapon we can find and have them set out to easy hand. If our four-legged friend comes a-visiting tonight, we'll meet him at those gates with his own weight in lead. We'll see how he deals with that.'

The colonel waved a hand. 'You must do as you think best,' he said. 'But I can't help feeling it's all a waste of time. How will you feel, Mr McCloud, if, after all this effort, nothing appears?'

'Relieved,' said Fraser. 'Obviously. But with respect, Colonel, you didn't see what we saw last night.'

Colonel Chivers glanced thoughtfully at Callum. 'The boy is staying too?' he asked.

'I've already told him he can leave if he wants to, but he has announced his intention to stay.' He looked at Callum. 'Last chance to change your mind,' he announced. 'If you do, I won't think any the worse of you.'

Callum considered for a moment and then shook his head.

'I'll stay,' he said. And for the first time, it felt like the right decision.

'Very well,' said Fraser. 'In that case, let's prepare ourselves.'

# 20

# SUNDOWN

The sun was rapidly setting in a great splash of crimson on the western horizon. Fraser and Callum stood on the long drive, surveying their handiwork. The gates were lashed tightly shut with as many lengths of chain as they could salvage from the stables. A short distance from them, lying in neatly ordered ranks at regular intervals along the drive, were dozens of rifles and pistols, each one of which had been meticulously primed and loaded, ready to fire.

Callum found himself counting the weapons and when he had finished, he'd arrived at the figure of twenty-six. Surely, he told himself, no creature, not even the fearful thing he'd seen at the Shepherd's Crook last night, could withstand such a formidable array of weaponry.

'If the beast appears,' murmured Fraser, 'and it somehow manages to get through that barrier . . .' He pointed to the gate. '. . . just put as many shots into it as you can. Don't hesitate, lad, don't wait for my permission to fire. Just make sure I'm not standing in the way when you pull the trigger. And, if it transpires that we cannot hold it back any longer, that's when we'll retreat to the house and take refuge within.' He pointed to the half-open front door behind them. The colonel had disappeared inside some hours ago and there'd been no sign of him since then.

Around midday, as they worked on the drive, he'd leant out of an upstairs window and shouted down to them that if they were hungry, they should help themselves to anything they wanted from the pantry. They had needed no second bidding. They'd entered the house and walked slowly along its grand corridors, gazing up at the massive oil paintings, the fine chandeliers, the opulent wallpapers and polished furniture. Not quite sure of their way, they found themselves wandering from room to room, staring open-mouthed at everything they saw. One massive chamber, its walls hung with richly woven tapestries, contained nothing but a grand piano and what appeared to be a spacious dance floor.

'This must be where the colonel used to host his fine parties,' said Fraser.

'Imagine all these rooms for just one person to live in,' murmured Callum. 'What must that be like?'

'Lonely, I imagine,' said Fraser. 'Andrew told me a wee bit about the colonel the night we arrived. He spent his whole youth in the army, travelling from country to country, from battle to battle. When all that was over, he took a young wife and built this place for the two of them to live in. But she took ill with a fever only a few months after they'd moved in and died soon after.'

'Ah, that's a shame,' said Callum.

'He took it hard, Andrew said. He never remarried, but instead, lived the life of a bachelor. His parties were legendary, and he used to host massive hunting trips into the forest, but over the past few years, his friends have stopped visiting him. I suppose they got older themselves. Some died, some became too infirm to travel . . . that's the way of old age. I suppose that's why he was planning to build that new hunting lodge, trying to entice younger acquaintances to come and spend some time with him . . .' He waved a hand around. 'I suppose all this is where his memories are. Little wonder he won't leave the place.'

'Do you really think that after everything that's happened, he still doesn't believe that the *Cù Sìth* exists?'

'If he doesn't, then he thinks we're both liars . . . or madmen.'

'I almost wish that was the case,' admitted Callum. 'But we both saw the thing that took Andrew, didn't we?'

Fraser nodded. 'I don't think I'll ever forget seeing it,' he murmured.

They finally located the kitchen and, right next to it, a pantry generously laden with food. The two of them dined on bread and cheese and slices of cold meat, cut straight from the bone, then washed it down with a mug of ale apiece. They took their time, enjoying every mouthful before retracing their steps and heading back to their work.

Now, as the sun sank all too rapidly beyond the horizon, and the long shadow of night began to stretch itself like a giant hand across the landscape, Callum remembered to be afraid. The time slipped leadenly by, and the darkness gradually deepened. They lit a couple of lanterns, sat down on the front steps and talked about whatever came into their heads. In the house, candles were lit and at one point Callum caught a glimpse of the colonel moving past a window, carrying a lamp, but that was the only sign they had that there was anyone at home.

As the clock moved steadily towards midnight, Callum began to feel a powerful tiredness tugging at his senses.

'Perhaps we should take turns to keep watch,' suggested Fraser. 'We could have an hour on and an hour off. If one of us goes inside, we—'

He broke off as a hair-raising sound reached them from somewhere across the moor – a prolonged, mournful howl rising on the air. Immediately, both Callum and Fraser snapped into wakefulness and got themselves upright. Callum stamped his feet, which were tingling with pins and needles.

'Do you think that was the beast?' he asked fearfully.

'It seems likely,' said Fraser. He walked along the drive to the nearest cluster of weapons and picked up a flintlock rifle. He peered up towards the gates, but they were too distant to make out very much detail. 'Let's have a closer look,' he suggested, and started walking. Callum followed, picking up another rifle as he did so, remembering to keep it pointed towards the ground as he followed Fraser. They had taken some ten steps when another howl sounded, closer this time, Callum thought, but still the gates were obscured by the gloom. Fraser quickened his pace, fell into a jog and Callum stayed with him. They made it to the gates and peered intently through the metal bars, but the moon was currently obscured by clouds and they could see very little out there. Callum pushed his face up close to the bars, struggling to make out detail, and then felt his blood chill in his veins as something big raced from left to right across his sightline some twenty yards ahead of him. He let out an involuntary gasp.

'What is it?' asked Fraser. 'Did you see something?'

Callum turned his head to reply, then lurched involuntarily backwards as something huge slammed against the metal gate, inches away from him, making the stone surround shudder to its foundations. He caught a glimpse of sharp white teeth flashing and heard a feral growl from beside the bars – then Fraser jammed the barrel of his rifle though a gap and pulled the trigger. There was a bright flash and the roar of the gun discharging was instantly followed by a high-pitched yelp. Fraser bared his own teeth.

'Yes, you felt that, didn't you?' he cried triumphantly. 'Maybe you're not impervious to lead after all!'

He spun around, ran back to the nearest loaded weapon and exchanged it for the spent one. Callum managed to steel himself to stay beside the gates and again was aware of something running across in front of him, a lithe furry shape. He jammed his own rifle into a gap, took quick aim and squeezed the trigger. The stock of the weapon bucked against his shoulder and in the flash of gunpowder, he had a momentary image of a huge, long-haired beast racing by – but he thought the creature jolted as the bullet ploughed into its flank. Perhaps, Callum told himself, this creature could be vanquished after all! He pulled the rifle back inside, dropped it to the ground and ran to fetch a replacement.

He was still stooping to pick up a new rifle when the gate was hit headlong a second time, with an impact that rocked it several feet out of alignment. Callum spun around with a gasp, looking fearfully up to the top of the gates, terrified they were about to come tumbling down on him. Fraser gestured frantically. 'Fall back a little,' he said. 'But be ready to fire again!'

Callum did as he was told, the two of them moving slowly backwards, eyes fixed to the gates. There was a deep silence and for a moment, Callum wondered if the beast had given up . . . but no sooner had the thought blossomed in his head, than the gate was hit a third time. And this time Callum caught a glimpse of what had struck it. He saw a huge head, hunched shoulders, a lolling tongue – and then the beast was gone again.

'That gate is going to fall,' murmured Fraser, sounding incredibly calm under the circumstances – and sure enough, the whole construction began to tip sideways, the metal foundations letting out an eerie groaning sound as they lost their grip in the earth. And then, quite suddenly, the gate was falling, emitting an ear-splitting din as it came down, flinging up chunks of masonry and emitting a long, grinding clamour. Callum and Fraser just managed to scramble clear of it as it slammed to the ground with an almighty crash. Dust billowed up, obscuring everything, and then slowly began to settle. Callum stared straight ahead, seeing but not wanting to see what had vanquished those mighty gates.

Moving forward over the fallen metal and scattered stones, great paws splayed, red eyes fixed on the two humans that waited . . . were three creatures.

# 21
# THE LAST STAND

*One for each person here.*

The thought flashed unbidden across Callum's mind and he tried to push it away. He did not want to dwell on the thought.

'Keep moving backwards,' said Fraser, through gritted teeth. 'And fire as you go.'

Callum nodded grimly. He remembered that he was holding a loaded rifle and snapped the gun up to take aim, putting the sights on the nearest of the three creatures, the one in the middle.

'Aim between the eyes,' he heard Fraser say, and Callum made a slight adjustment before squeezing the trigger. The impact of the lead shot stopped the creature in its tracks and Callum actually saw the bullet slam into its skull, punching a sizable hole in its cranium. Callum held his breath, hoping that this shot would do the trick . . . but the beast didn't fall. It shook its head, as though trying to dispel an ache, and then it came on again, moving slowly like its companions, clearly in no great hurry to end this. Callum and Fraser had no option but to keep retreating, firing a round, stooping to pick up a fresh weapon and ensuring that every shot found its target. But the hounds did no more than hesitate for a few moments before prowling onwards, their heads close to the ground, their blazing red eyes intent on their prey.

Callum began to accept that he and Fraser were doomed. Not one shot was doing what it was supposed to, and now they were drawing close to the main doors of the house and only a few loaded weapons remained. Callum thought about his parents, who might never find out what happened to their son, and he felt a terrible sadness settle over him. And yet, some stubborn part of him clung on to the vague hope that the next shot he took would be the one to change things. Or the next . . .

And then he became aware of movement behind him. He allowed himself to glance back and saw to his astonishment that a figure was marching out of the house on to the front step. It was Colonel Chivers and, for reasons best known only to himself, he was dressed in his army uniform, his medals glinting proudly on the lapel of his red jacket. He was holding what looked like a cutlass and he studied Callum and Fraser as though inspecting ranks of armed men waiting to go into battle. The steely gleam in his eye suggested he was not of sound mind.

'Prepare yourselves, gentlemen!' he roared. 'The honour of the regiment is at stake. Sell your lives dearly!'

And then, raising the cutlass high in the air, he gave a powerful roar and ran forward. Both Callum and Fraser reacted a little too late, lunging towards the old man to try and restrain him, but he evaded their grasp and ran straight at the nearest hound. He lifted his cutlass and brought the blade straight down on to its shoulders, the sharp steel biting deep into flesh. Callum really didn't want to see what happened next but somehow couldn't bring himself to shut his eyes.

The hound reacted with a roar of anger. It reared up and leapt forward, its huge jaws snapping around the old man's neck like a steel trap. He was jerked clean off his feet, his skinny legs kicking frantically. In one lithe movement, the creature whipped around and raced back towards the gates, taking the colonel's uniformed figure with it.

Callum heard Fraser yell something and he raised his own rifle but knew he didn't dare fire at the departing hound in case the bullet found the old man instead. He watched helplessly as the beast raced along the drive, leapt over the fallen gates and carried the colonel's body off into the darkness.

The other two hounds stood where they were for a moment, as if deliberating their next move – and Callum experienced a brief surge of hope, thinking that perhaps they would be satisfied now that they had the Colonel. But, no, they started prowling forward again, each of them regarding its intended victim. Callum could feel the glare of the creature on the left looking at him with merciless intent, while the other fixed its red eyes on Fraser, who gave a defiant roar of anger and unleashed a shot at almost point-blank range. The hound jolted as the bullet struck it in the throat and it stood for a moment, shaking its head. Then it moved on again, intent on claiming what it had come for. Fraser let the smoking rifle drop from his hands. He turned his head to look at Callum and the boy could see that all the fight had suddenly drained out of him, as though he had finally accepted that the game was finally up. His shoulders slumped, he stared intently at Callum and croaked a single word. 'Run,' he said.

'But . . .'

'I said, run, damn you! Can't you see, we cannot hope to beat them? Try and hide in the house, perhaps they will spare you.'

'But I can't leave you!'

'Do it, boy. It's my fault you're here. Just—'

But then the nearest hound was upon him, leaping up from behind and enclosing Fraser's neck in its powerful jaws. Callum saw his employer's face register the agony of the moment, but he still somehow managed to form one final scream. 'RUN!'

And then Fraser was whirled off his feet, as though he weighed no more than a straw man, and the hound was carrying him triumphantly towards the gates, Fraser kicking and struggling to no avail. For an instant, Callum considered following but realised that it would be pointless. There was nothing he could do. As he watched, frozen, the hound carried Fraser away into the darkness.

Callum dropped his own rifle. The remaining hound studied him in silence for a moment as though considering what to do. Its red eyes glittered malevolently, then seemed to focus. It emitted a deep, rumbling growl and started forward again.

Callum's nerve finally broke. He spun on his heel and, intent now only on his own survival, he ran for the open door of the house.

# 22

# AND THEN THERE WAS ONE

In seconds he was up the steps, across the threshold and slamming the heavy door shut behind him, pausing for a moment to slide a solid wooden bar across the frame. Something clattered against his foot and, looking down, he saw a fancy flintlock pistol lying on the floor, probably something that the colonel had dropped on his way out. Callum stooped, swept the pistol up into one hand and began to run along the corridor, searching for somewhere he might find sanctuary.

An instant later, he heard the sound of the door behind him being hit by incredible force and glancing fearfully back, he saw that the solid wood was bulging against its frame as though a battering ram was being taken to it.

Callum could hardly breathe he was so scared, but he somehow managed to convince his feet to keep carrying him along the corridor, past the massive paintings and handsome statues, deeper into the labyrinth of Chivers Hall. A wide doorway offered itself on his right and he plunged through it, finding himself in some kind of a drawing room, with leather chairs and finely polished wooden tables, but there was no obvious place to hide here, so he kept going, horribly aware of the sound of splintering wood from the direction of the front door. The beast was still intent on coming after him, it would be inside in moments!

Another doorway straight ahead beckoned and he plunged through it, finding himself in a hallway with a huge curving staircase ahead of him. He pounded up the stairs, hardly pausing for breath, telling himself the hound would have less purchase on those shiny wooden steps and that this might just prove to be an advantage. He heard what must have been the final crash as the front door was shattered into pieces, but kept on climbing.

He made it to the top of the stairs and stood for a moment in an agony of indecision, unsure of which way to go, but after a moment's hesitation, he went left and raced along a wide landing. Glancing over the bannister rail, he saw to his horror that the hound was already racing madly through the drawing room below, its claws skittering and sliding on wooden floorboards. It blundered into a table, knocking the thing over with a loud crash, and then it paused for a moment to sniff the air with its huge nostrils. Its ears twitched as it caught the sound of Callum's feet clumping on floorboards overhead and it moved on again, looking for the staircase.

Up on the landing, a closed door beckoned on his right and Callum flung it open and raced into the room beyond, slamming the door behind him. He stood for a moment, gasping for breath, looking frantically around. He was standing in a small bedroom, which contained a four-poster bed, a dressing table and a chair. To his horror, he realised that there appeared to be no other door leading out of here. He was trapped. He turned back towards the door but heard the sound of paws clacking along the landing towards him and realised that it was too late to try and leave by that route. He looked frantically around and realised that his only possible escape was via the window. He ran to it, looked out and saw the driveway with its ranks of discarded weapons directly below him. He reached up and tried the handle of the window, but it seemed to be stuck fast, no matter how hard he tried to twist it – and from the other side of the door, there came that hideous rumbling growl as the beast sensed his presence.

There was no time to waste. He used the heavy butt of the pistol like a hammer on the metal handle of the window and managed to twist it around. He flung the window wide and began to clamber up onto the sill. Almost instantly, the bedroom door was struck by a powerful blow, the wood bulging from the impact. Callum didn't hesitate. He thrust his legs through the open window and pushed himself out. He dropped through the air. His feet struck the ground, the impact sending jolts of pain through his knees, but he performed an ungainly forward roll and came awkwardly back to his feet. He glanced up towards the window, saw a hideous hairy face framed in the opening and started to run along the drive, thinking that if he could just get past those fallen gates, then perhaps he might have a chance of losing the creature out on the moor in the darkness.

Seconds later, there was the sound of smashing glass and then he heard the thud of the beast landing heavily just behind him. He put his head down and ran as hard as he could, determined to create some distance between himself and his pursuer – but he hadn't taken enough notice of the discarded weapons littering the drive. A rifle got in the way, tripping him, and he went face down in a sprawl on the ground. For a moment, he lay there, stunned, telling himself it was all over for him – that it was futile to fight this any longer – but at the last instant something made him scramble up on to his knees. The pistol was still clutched like a talisman in his right hand and he extended one shaking arm as the brute slowed to a walk and came towards him, its nostrils flared, savouring the smell of his fear. Callum aimed the pistol between the creature's eyes, offered up a silent prayer and pulled the trigger.

There was a dry click as the hammer fell.

Callum gasped, realising that the gun hadn't even been loaded. He let it drop from his shaking hand and kneeled where he was, waiting to die. He could see the hound now in every hideous detail – its matted, dark greenish fur, it's wolf-like ears, its blazing crimson eyes. He could see the jagged teeth jutting down from under its lips and all the places where bullets had ploughed into the creature, leaving pitted bloodless marks in its body. The hound readied itself for the final leap. Its lips curled back to reveal those yellow teeth. It bunched its muscles ready to spring . . .

'No!' The voice came from right behind Callum, startling him, and he recognised it instantly. He turned his head to look in astonishment. Mhairi was standing a short distance away, gazing fearlessly down at the hound – one hand extended, the palm raised as if issuing an instruction. 'You have the wrong man,' she said. 'He is not your enemy.'

Bewildered, Callum turned back to look at the hound and saw a puzzled expression in those brutish eyes, saw the lips droop back to cover the teeth.

'Do you hear me?' asked Mhairi. 'Those that have already been taken are vengeance enough.' Now she moved closer and sank to her knees beside Callum. She slipped an arm protectively around his shoulders. 'You mustn't fear,' she told the hound.

'We will make amends for everything that has been done. This is my promise to you and to the walkers. The boy beside me will also help to set things right. Listen . . .' She leant closer, as if to confide a secret. 'We will replant all the trees that were destroyed, every last one of them. The sacred circle will be hidden once more from the world and I promise – we both promise – that this work will be undertaken soon, within days. If I do not keep my word, you may come for me and I shall go gladly.'

Callum looked from Mhairi to the beast and back again, noting to his astonishment that some kind of understanding really did seem to be passing between them. And then Mhairi spoke again, and Callum wondered if perhaps he was dreaming this part, because the words were not in any kind of language he had heard before. It was a strange, lilting dialect; one that seemed to have a calming effect on the creature. All of the anger seemed to fade from its features in an instant. It dropped back on to its haunches and listened as she talked, its head tilted slightly to one side, but the red eyes still seemed to have a look of inquiry about them.

The hound seemed to be waiting for something.

'Make it an offering,' murmured Mhairi.

Callum looked at her. 'What?' he whispered.

'It wants something from you. Some kind of sacrifice. Give it something . . . a coin, a keepsake, anything you've got.'

'But, I don't have . . .' Callum slipped his hands into the pockets of his jacket and the fingers of his right hand felt something cold and hard to the touch. He withdrew whatever it was and found he was clutching Wee Davie, the soldier's painted face smiling calmly up at him. Callum glanced at Mhairi enquiringly and she gave him a nod. He extended his arm, hand open, the lead soldier lying on the flat of his palm. The hound moved its head closer and sniffed quizzically at Wee Davie, then took the offering carefully, almost delicately, in its mouth.

Then Mhairi was getting to her feet and helping Callum to do the same.

'Now,' she whispered calmly. 'We'll leave, shall we?'

Callum stared at her, open-mouthed. 'What . . . what just happened?' he whispered. 'What exactly did you say to it?'

'Let's talk about that later,' she suggested and started to lead him along the drive towards the fallen gates. He glanced fearfully over his shoulder. The hound was still lying there, watching them calmly but making no effort to follow. Callum looked back towards the gates and now he saw the white shape of Blizzard waiting there for them.

'What about Molly?' he whispered. 'I left her in the stables.'

'I think we'll come back for her later,' said Mhairi. 'Right now, we need to – oh!'

She had just sensed movement behind them. Callum held his breath, aware that the hound was back on its feet and was approaching them. They both froze in their tracks, but the hound went right past them at a brisk trot, heading for the gates. Blizzard flared his nostrils and stamped his feet, spooked by the creature's proximity, but it ignored him and went on by into the darkness of the moor.

Callum remembered to breathe. He looked at Mhairi, bewildered. He recalled what had happened before she got there.

'Fraser . . .' he whispered. '. . . and the colonel, they both . . .'

She nodded. 'It was always going to happen,' she said.

'There was nothing I could do for them. But *you* didn't deserve the same fate. You were only doing as you were ordered. I think there was some confusion there, for a while, but in the end, they understood.'

'They?'

'The walkers,' she said, as if that explained everything. 'But you heard what I promised them, Callum. The replanting. It has to be done, and soon, or they'll come back. And if they come again, there'll be no second chances.'

He nodded. He thought he understood what she was saying. They clambered over the shattered remains of the gate and Mhairi climbed into Blizzard's saddle. She reached down a hand to help Callum up behind her. He got himself into position and put his arms tight around her waist. Mhairi clicked her heels into Blizzard's flanks and they moved off at a walk. Callum looked back at the empty house.

'What will happen to that place now?' he murmured.

She shrugged her shoulders. 'Your guess is as good as mine,' she said. 'But I don't really care. In time, perhaps the trees will cover it.'

She urged Blizzard into a canter and they headed off across the dark moor in the direction of the Shepherd's Crook.

# EPILOGUE

Callum and Mhairi rode their horses to the ridge and looked down at the cleared land where most of the inhabitants of the village were hard at work, digging the soil and planting saplings. They had been dug up from the most remote places in the forest and brought by the barrow load to be replanted in the naked ground around the faerie circle. For every tree that had been cut down, there would eventually be a bright green sapling set in the space between the stumps.

After two weeks of intensive work, where everybody able to lift a spade had helped, the hard edges left by the woodcutters were already beginning to blur into a softer green. Of course, it would take years to hide the circle as it had once been hidden, but the process was begun and that was the important thing. And there had been no more attacks since that last night at Chivers Hall, no more disappearances. It was beginning to feel as though the ordeal really was over.

Callum had stayed all that time at the inn, dividing his efforts between working out by the forest's edge and helping with the renovations at the Shepherd's Crook. Mhairi was intent on returning the place to its former glory, and already the staff had come back to lend a hand and the first guests were beginning to book their places. But Callum had something on his mind.

'When will you leave?' Mhairi asked him now and he glanced at her guiltily, wondering how it was that she always knew what was on his mind.

'In a wee while,' he muttered. 'How did you know?'

'You packed up all your things in that saddle bag,' she said, not looking at him. 'I must say, I'm sorry. I thought you were happy here.'

'I am. I have been. But . . . well, my parents will have had no word of me. They'll want to know I'm alive and well. And . . . I thought I should call and see Mother McCloud; tell her what happened to Fraser.'

Now Mhairi did look at him. 'What will you tell her?' she asked him.

'Not the truth,' he admitted. 'She'll think I'm off my head. But I thought I should give her the money that we found in his room. That should be safe enough to do, don't you think?'

Mhairi nodded and returned her gaze to the scene below. 'I should get down there and lend them a hand,' she said. 'I'll be accused of shirking, since all this was my idea.'

'It's a brilliant idea,' Callum assured her. 'And I love the way you talked them into doing it.'

She looked at him again, and now he saw a yearning look in those pale red eyes. 'Will you come back and see me again?' she asked him.

'Of course I will,' he assured her. 'Soon enough. Like I said, I just want to see my parents and let them know that all is well with me.'

'I wonder who will look after you on your travels,' she murmured. 'Now that Wee Davie is gone.' And with that, she urged Blizzard over the crest of the hill and rode slowly down to join the others. Callum watched her for a few moments, feeling torn at the thought of leaving her. But in the end, he turned Molly away and started riding.

***

He had gone perhaps five miles or so when he recognised the landscape he was riding through; and he wasn't exactly surprised when he heard a voice singing a familiar refrain.

> *'Poor Johnny lies a-sleepin'*
> *The moonlight comes a-creepin'*
> *And all his children gather now*
> *To say their last goodbyes . . .'*

Callum felt the blood slow in his veins. He looked around, over the brow of a low hill, and saw a familiar shingle bank beside a gently winding river. The old woman was kneeling by the water, washing clothes. He looked down at her for a very long time, thinking about riding on, but he was somehow unable to bring himself to do it. He knew only too well that it was no coincidence she was waiting for him here.

Eventually, he climbed down from the saddle. He tethered Molly to a nearby tree and walked slowly down to the river, the old woman's voice filling his head as he moved slowly closer, his feet crunching on loose stones. Soon enough, he was standing right behind her, looking over her shoulder and watching as her webbed hands moved a blue shirt rhythmically back and forth in the flow

189

of the water. He couldn't be sure, but he thought it looked like the spare shirt he had put into his pack only that morning.

He swallowed and was glad to note that nothing sinister seemed to be coming out of the fabric, no traces of blood – and now that he looked closer, he wasn't even sure it *was* his shirt, the buttons were surely a different colour.

'So, you didn't stay long,' said the woman, without looking up. 'Heading homewards so soon?'

'Aye,' said Callum. 'I thought I should.'

'Such a sad state of affairs in your home village.'

'Sad?' He watched her hands working on the fabric.

'Oh yes. Didn't you hear. Those two whose son recently left them . . . such a tragedy there was. A fire. They say the husband was steeped in drink one night and knocked over a lantern as his wife slept. At any rate, it was the end of them.'

'Both of them?' whispered Callum, his voice brittle with dread.

'Aye.' The woman gave a long sigh. 'So sad. Every night, the woman wept for her son, but her husband thought the boy was better off gone. He told his wife he had plans to win money in a card game and when he had done that, then he would be able to pay off his debt and get the boy back. But of course, he never won a single game.'

'Both gone,' murmured Callum. 'I see.'

The old woman shook her head. 'Such fools, they are, these people, with their dreams and their hopes.' Now she turned her head and looked up at him, just her grey eyes visible above the shroud that covered her face. 'I could have told them,' she said, 'that their boy was better off now - that he had found a new home, with someone who loves him . . . somebody who will watch over him all the days of his life. But of course, I never had the opportunity to speak to them and now it's too late.'

She went back to her mournful song and carried on with her work.

Callum watched her in silence for a few moments, aware of the hot tears coursing down his cheeks. Then he dashed them from his eyes with the sleeve of his jacket and turned away. He walked back up the bank to Molly and clambered up into the saddle. He sat in silence for a moment, thinking hard and watching the flow of the river as it wound its way into the distance. Perhaps, he told himself, the washer had been speaking of *other* parents, not his - but he knew deep in his heart that she'd been telling him the truth, and that there was no point in going back to look for them.

Finally, he turned Molly around and started back the way he had come.

***

When he returned to the place where he had left Mhairi, he saw her down by the faerie circle, working amongst the other villagers, planting yet another sapling. He climbed down from the saddle, secured Molly alongside Blizzard and walked out amongst the tree stumps until he was standing beside Mhairi. She worked on and didn't look up at him.

'Forget something?' she asked him.

He shook his head and got to his knees beside her. 'I got to thinking about what you said,' he murmured. 'About not having Wee Davie to look after me. I thought I'd come back here and see if you had another lead soldier I could keep in my pocket.'

She stopped what she was doing and looked up at him, a wry smile on her face. She brought up a hand, muddy with fresh earth and took his hand in hers. 'You won't need him if you stick with me,' she said. 'I'll look after you in Davie's place. How would that be?'

'Sounds like a plan,' he admitted.

'Good.' She released him. 'Now, since you're here, why don't you make yourself useful?' She pointed to a nearby barrow. 'There's another sapling in there,' she said. 'Will you bring it to me?'

'I will,' he said. 'If you make me a promise.'

She seemed amused by that. 'That depends on what it is,' she said.

'The language you spoke to the hound that night at the hall. Will you teach me to speak it?'

'We'll see,' she said. She gestured impatiently. 'The sapling?'

'You have to promise first,' he insisted.

She thought for a moment. 'I promise I'll try,' she told him. 'How's that?'

'I suppose it'll have to do,' he said, and getting to his feet he went to the barrow to fetch her the sapling.


## THE END

# IF YOU LIKE THIS, YOU'LL LOVE . . .

*'A great read. The Witching Stone is spooky, funny and occasionally well gross, with an ancient mystery at its core.'*
Charlie Higson

'Brimful of nostalgia and cinematic atmosphere.
A thrilling read and a clever new twist on
the vampire stories you love.'
Laura Wood

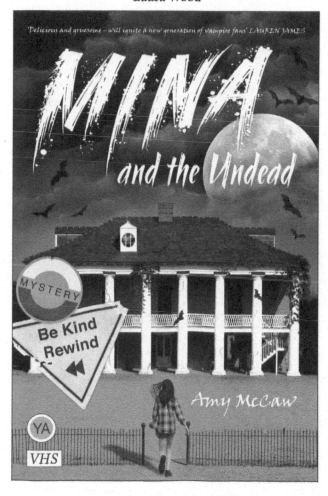

'Delicious and gruesome – will ignite a new generation of vampire fans' LAUREN JAMES

MINA

and the Undead

MYSTERY

Be Kind
Rewind
◀◀

YA

VHS

Amy McCaw

Where sinister beings stir and tormented souls seek revenge.
What if survival relied on facing your greatest fears?

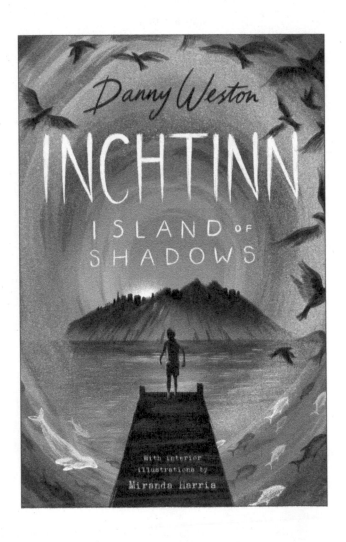

Danny Weston

INCHTINN

ISLAND OF
SHADOWS

With interior
illustrations by
Miranda Harris

Not even the dead are safe . . .

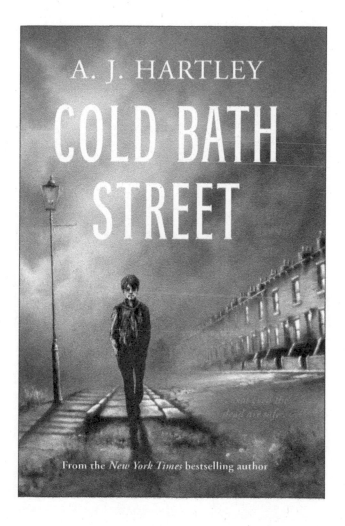

A. J. HARTLEY

COLD BATH
STREET

From the *New York Times* bestselling author

In the Monster Belt, discoveries are made.
Some good, some bad, some life changing.

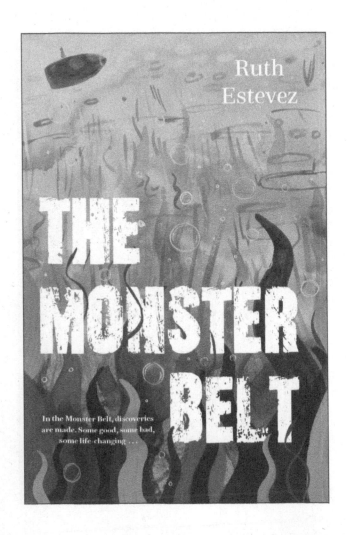

A psychological horror that will grip you
from the first page, and haunt you long
after you've finished the last.

# ACKNOWLEDGMENTS

As ever, there are people to thank - Hazel Holmes and the team at UCLan Publishing, Kathy Webb for the insightful copy editing and Amy Cooper who did the brilliant cover design. But this year there are many others who deserve a mention.

This book was conceived and created during the COVID 19 pandemic and I retreated to the eighteenth century for my setting, thinking I'd be far away from all that. It was only after finishing that it occured to me that I may just have written an allegory all about it.

And of course, there are so many people who kept me going through this strange and difficult year.

As ever, Susan Singfield tops the list for her constant help, advice and encouragement, but there are more: the people at Zoom Communications, for instance, who made it possible for me to stay in touch with friends throughout the pandemic and even allowed me to do some virtual school visits.

Thanks to the wonderful authors at Writers, Inc., who reminded me how important it is to get regular feedback on work - and just how much I'd missed the group since leaving Manchester.

Thanks to the young authors at The Writers' Den, who filled me with so much hope for the future - and to the many members of the Edinburgh Writers' Salon, who were kind enough to include me in their recent anthology, Lost, Looking and Found.

Thanks to Louise and David at Tasty Buns and the team at Mary's Milk Bar for providing delicious food for thought.

Thanks to Lucy Wyndham-Read, whose online workouts helped keep me trim, when eating delicious food was one of the few pleasures to be found. I mustn't forget to thank the team at the No Such Thing As a Fish podcast whose output has kept me entertained and informed on a nightly basis.

Thanks to The Eco Larder for plastic-free supplies and to Shrub, for making the weekly budget go further in a planet-conscious way. Thanks to the team at Dig-In, who provided a weekly delivery of vegetables and to The Meadows for being where it is, providing a handy place for my morning walks. Thanks to The Cameo Cinema Bar, our regular home from home, for opening up again and bringing back some semblance of normality. Thanks to the NHS for administering vaccines in an orderly fashion - to all those unknown people who worked to create it in the first place - and thanks to Bob and Brenda, who demonstrated how to keep going in the face of real adversity.

And finally, thanks to you.

Yes, you, reading this. Give yourself a pat on the back for picking up *A Hunter's Moon* and, in so doing, providing this writer with another reason to get up in the morning. It means a lot.

# HAVE YOU EVER WONDERED HOW BOOKS ARE MADE?

UCLan Publishing is an award winning independent publisher specialising in Children's and Young Adult books. Based at The University of Central Lancashire, this Preston based publisher teaches MA Publishing students how to become industry professionals using the content and resources from its business; students are included at every stage of the publishing process and credited for the work that they contribute.

The business doesn't just help publishing students though. UCLan Publishing has supported the employability and real-life work skills for the university's Illustration, Acting, Translation, Animation, Photography, Film & TV students and many more. This is the beauty of books and stories; they fuel many other creative industries! The MA Publishing students are able to get involved from day one with the business and they acquire a behind the scenes experience of what it is like to work for a such a reputable independent.

The MA course was awarded a Times Higher Award (2018) for Innovation in the Arts and the business, UCLan Publishing, was awarded Best Newcomer at the Independent Publishing Guild (2019) for the ethos of teaching publishing using a commercial publishing house. As the business continues to grow, so to does the student experience upon entering this dynamic Masters course.

www.uclanpublishing.com
www.uclanpublishing.com/courses/
uclanpublishing@uclan.ac.uk